Tales from 1492

by

Mary Ann Whittier

FOURTH PRINTING

Royal Fireworks Press
Unionville, New York

Royal Fireworks Press
First Avenue, PO Box 399
Unionville, NY 10988-0399
(845) 726-4444
FAX: (845) 726-3824
email: rfpress@frontiernet.net

ISBN: 0-89824-980-5

Printed in the United States of America on acid-free, recycled paper using soy-based inks by the Royal Fireworks Printing Company of Unionville New York.

Illustrations

Author's Note

I am thankful for the many factors which contributed to this book. The historical events and characters provided inspiration; encouragement and support came from family and friends; the librarians and resources at Stanford University, the Huntington Library, the Pierpont Morgan Library, and local libraries in San Clemente and Sunnyvale, California were invaluable. Special thanks go to JoAnn Kuhn for early encouragement, and to Mark Blencowe, whose sense of history, understanding and intelligence helped me to bring this book to final form.

Tales from 1492 with its week to week format began to take shape in 1985. A broken femur that January led to a restricted contemplative year in which I began research and writing. By December my leg was as good as new, and I had learned that one year and one event in that year can alter history. As my husband, Bob, pointed out, "If I hadn't taken you skiing, you wouldn't have written this book." True, and today I feel more inclined to write another book than to ski. Bob encourages both.

Meeting famous people of 1492 and some fictional characters in accurate surroundings should help the reader to enjoy politics, art, and discoveries. I hope that a global view of that one year can be a starting point for the reader to become Hooked on History.

Imagine watching CNN in 1492. Impossible, of course. But communication in the 15th century was experiencing a revolution comparable to that of television news in the 20th century. The printed book in Europe was a growing industry, literacy was on the rise, the wisdom of the ancient Greeks and Romans was appearing in public libraries. Europe was way behind China where printed books appeared 400 years earlier. In the New World, the Mayans hand copied their extensive libraries.

If your FAX machine or computer modem gave you reports from around the world in 1492, their compilation might be this book.

Fourteen Hundred Ninety Two was the year when the Old World met the New World as Christopher Columbus sailed three small ships of Spaniards across the Atlantic Ocean. Columbus thought he'd reached the islands off the coast of Japan and China, the Indies, and he called the Native Americans he met Indians.

Why were Europeans attracted to China and Japan? Marco Polo's travels there 200 years ago had not been forgotten. The growing Moslem influence had closed the old silk routes to China. So, while Popes continued to appoint a Catholic Archbishop of Peking (Beijing), none of the appointees had been able to arrive at his diocese for more than a century. Shiite and Sunnite Moslems fought with each other, but also controlled much of eastern Europe, Jerusalem, Cairo, parts of the Indian sub-continent and Malaysia. Only in Spain did Islam suffer a defeat. In 1492, Isabella and Ferdinand followed their victory over the last Moslem Sultan with the expulsion of the Jews.

Portuguese ships aimed for China by going around Africa, and in the process, they sailed up the Congo River and exchanged ambassadors and goods with the great Bantu kingdom. China itself was flourishing under their Ming Emperor. Their new capital in the north provided security, and they welcomed isolation.

Today, successful, productive people are frequently specialists. In 1492, science, art, religion, and philosophy were intertwined. Several schools and universities we know today were just receiving second generation students. Leonardo da Vinci, admired as the Renaissance man for his broad interests, was 40 and working in Milan.

Many of the settings for this book may be enjoyed by tourists today: the Forbidden City of Beijing, Windsor Castle, the Alhambra in Granada, Topkapi Palace in Istanbul, and Hawaii's City of Refuge. Others have disappeared; old Canton was torn down in this century. Some environmentalists existed in the New World, but in Europe, chamber pots were emptied in the streets. Today, you can visit the Kremlin, which Ivan the Great was building in 1492, but you won't be able to see great flocks of parrots that once filled the skies over Cuba.

Europe was finally recovering from the ravages of the Black Death. Outbreaks of the plague would continue to occur over the next three centuries, but stability had returned. The independent city-states of the Italian Peninsula, Naples, Florence, Urbino and Milan among others, were striving to recapture the power of Rome by reanimating its arts and letters. Latin was the language of scholars throughout the continent. German cities, such as Augsberg, Nuremberg and Mainz, were reviving trade and expanding their spheres of influence north into the Oceanvs Germanicvs, the Baltic and North Seas. Roman Catholicism was the Church of Europe, challenged only around its eastern edge by the Orthodox Christians who were reestablishing themselves after the fall of Constantinople 40 years before.

The royal families of England, France and Spain fought, intermarried, and negotiated to establish nations out of feudal fiefdoms. Ninety percent of the people were farmers. A large city contained 20,000 people; the total European population was about 100,000,000. Winters and summers had grown cooler over the past century and a half. Many harbors of Iceland and Greenland were clogged with ice, hampering trade. Vineyards in southern England had died out and been abandoned by 1492.

A new age was dawning, and this is the story of people, places and events of its initial year. Was 1492 special? It is probably one date in history that most Americans can identify. What was Europe like when Columbus left on his voyage? How were the "Indians" of North and South America living? Who was ruling? What beautiful things were being created in India, China, Japan and Africa? Some people living in 1492 have familiar names like Michelangelo, Martin Luther, Nicolaus Copernicus, Babar the Mongol, Montezuma the Aztec, Lucretia Borgia, Albrecht Dürer and Christopher Columbus, who was known as Cristóbal Colón in Spain. Others, like Casimir of Poland, the

Inca Huayna Cápac, the Bantu ruler Mani Kongo, the Spanish sailor Martin Pinzón, or the Ottoman Sultan Bayazid II, are also important threads in the fabric of 1492. It was a pivotal year for this world we live in. How different it is 500 years later! Or is it?

Mary Ann Whittier
December, 1990

January

Monday[1]

The tower keep of Windsor Castle looms above the morning fog and mist of the Thames River. Archers are no longer stationed behind the crenelated walls of the old fortress. On the four smaller towers, watchmen armed with pistols provide security for the royal family within. A knock on his door awakens Henry Tudor from the fitful sleep of a King who was not born to rule. Concerns with revolts and conspiracies flee from his mind as his chamberlain's reassuring voice begins the day with, "Happy New Year, Your Majesty!"

Behind the curtains of his bed, Henry yawns and stretches himself. His legs are sore from yesterday's long ride to the hounds. A servant adds a log to the embers in the fireplace and begins to prepare a shaving bowl. By the time the chamberlain crosses the room to draw the bed curtains, Henry's large hand has pulled them aside and his voice booms, "Good morning." For the 34 year old King of England, it is another day to defend his authority and finance his dynasty. But this first day of the year is also one for him to join his queen and his court to hear Mass.

When the year of our Lord 1492 dawned in England, the Holy Catholic Church was proclaiming the Feast of the Circumcision throughout Europe. More than 1000 years before, Popes St. Symmachus and St. Hormisdas had proclaimed this a holy day of obligation in an attempt to curtail pagan celebrations of the new year. Christians celebrated this event in the life of the Infant Jesus, who followed this ancient Jewish rite started with Abraham as a covenant between man and God. This feast day opened the liturgical year for Christians, Roman Catholic and Eastern Orthodox. As yet there were no reformers emphasizing Paul's letter to the Galatians 5:6, "For in Christ Jesus neither circumcision nor uncircumcision is of any avail, but faith working through love."

At Windsor Castle the priest is concluding the Mass in St. George's Chapel. The high ceilings in the Perpendicular Gothic style are supported by fan vaulting that is so delicate that it hardly seems carved of stone. The woodcarvers have included more charming, earthly scenes on the choir stalls. Even the carved canopies above each stall cannot approach the soaring beauty of the fans reaching toward heaven. The Queen finds security in this chapel built by her father Edward IV. In her sixth year of marriage, Elizabeth believes that her third child, the baby Henry, should be the one to serve the church.

As the royal entourage goes from Chapel to Audience Hall, the king identifies with William the Conqueror who built this fortress on the Thames more than 400 years ago. Henry Tudor is in his seventh year of power and also gained the throne in battle. From the parapets he can see Eton College, 51 years old and one of the few things from the rule of Henry VI which evokes English pride.

England was just emerging from more than a century of dynastic squabbles within its royal house and with the royal house of France. As an infant, Henry VI was crowned King of France and of England, at the cathedral of Nôtre Dame in Paris. His accession to the throne occurred at the premature death of his father, Henry V, who had conquered France and married the daughter of its king. The widowed Queen of England and France was married again to a Welshman named Owen Tudor, and was the grandmother of Henry Tudor. This Henry's ties to the English royal house were somewhat more obscure; in fact, he had a closer

3

claim to the French throne than to the English. But Henry Tudor had the best claim of all to the throne; he won it on the field of battle. More importantly he kept it by shrewd administration, which was not matched by his insipid Lancastrian uncle Henry VI, who lost France and England (twice), or by the boisterous Yorks, whose principles compared well to those of the Borgias. Henry Tudor married the Yorkist heir, Elizabeth, the daughter of Edward IV, hoping to cement his family's claim to the throne and end the years of bloodshed.

Henry VII and Elizabeth, King and Queen of England, appear in royal robes and crowns. They are elegant enough to inspire a picture of authority, but not so sumptuous as to dazzle their subjects; Henry keeps a close watch on the treasury. Members of the court present them with gifts for the new year. Lancasters and Yorks acknowledge the rule of this first Tudor King. The Wars of the Roses are over, and Henry means to unite these divided factions. For this New Year's audience, five year old Princess Margaret, three year old Prince Arthur, and the Infant Prince Henry are in attendance. As the heirs to both sides of the conflict, these children should evoke loyalty from the red rose of Lancaster and the white rose of York.

As Roman Emperors received gifts each new year, Henry is appropriating this tradition. The Earl of Warwick presents Henry with a ruby ring, Elizabeth with a pearl in a velvet box, and a silver porringer for the new baby. He has a book for Margaret and a toy boat for Arthur. When Bartolome Columbus presents Henry with embroidered leather riding gloves, he uses the opportunity to speak again on behalf of his older brother, Christopher.

"Great and noble King Henry, let this year be the time when you will commission my brother to sail West to China and Japan. For a small investment of a few ships

4

and men, Christopher will bring you the gold and pearls and spices of the Orient. These gifts today are but shadows of the riches that will be yours."

"Yes, yes," Henry replies absentmindedly, "we will speak of this at a more convenient time."

Tomorrow will bring chimney-sweeps to Windsor Castle, cleaning all the chimneys. Not only is this a safeguard against clogs and fires, but a symbol of a fresh start in a new year. Many an Englishman gives his wife pin money to buy the handmade pins needed for the year. Henry and Elizabeth observe these customs of their people, but Henry will hire a chimney-sweep and study the reports from France. Brittany's loyalty seems to be following their Princess Anne, the new bride of the French king, Charles VIII. It takes more than pin money to hold English territory across the channel.

Feast of the Circumcision

In San Marco Church, Sandro Botticelli lifts his eyes to his Coronation of the Virgin. He is painting a medley of cherubim, zephyrs and roses to surround Mary. They will lend a sweetness to the formal heavenly portrait, in which God, wearing the triple tiara of the Pope, holds a crown over the head of the bowing Virgin. After four months of work on this massive altar piece, Sandro knows there is still much to be done.

"I hope Savonarola's sermon isn't longer than an hour," Botticelli thinks. "I'd like to get to the scaffolding and complete the heavenly scene at the top before Lent begins." Sandro sits on the men's side of the curtain which divides San Marco. As a 46 year old bachelor, and a shy one at that, perhaps he feels more worshipful in this semi-monastic setting. When his eyes travel to his unfinished work, he thinks the roses simple compared to the botany he had mastered for his Primavera, but he wishes he might sit with the women and children to observe the innocent faces and dimpled hands he needs for his angels.

Fra. Girolamo Savonarola has a hooked nose and sunken eyes. His pasty skin and coarse Dominican habit complete his appearance. Yet this ugly, small, colorless priest exudes a saintly humility. "Yes," thinks Botticelli, "I must capture that saintly quality with the four saints at the bottom of my altar piece." Savonarola appears older than his 40 years, as if the world is sucking the life from him. But when he begins to preach, the fire of the reformer transforms him.

6

Famine and destruction were the monk's prediction of God's judgment on Florence, unless the city turned from worldly pleasures. His pious asceticism has not been a surprise to Lorenzo the Magnificent, but the crowds at his sermons are. Savonarola's Lenten sermons in Florence five years ago had been pedestrian; attendance had fallen to only a few dozen faithful at the end of his Lenten series. Now, after a year and a half at San Marco, he is attracting large attentive audiences. He preaches against the very worldliness the Medici personify: sending a younger son to the church for political advantage, keeping mistresses, encouraging the humanism of the classic Greeks and Romans, and self-indulgence in fine foods and clothing. He has proposed a remote and austere new building, where the clergy could be an example of renouncing earthly pleasures, but he resides at San Marco, a beautiful edifice of columns and frescoes. Its library is stocked by fabulous illuminated manuscripts donated by Cosimo de Medici. A bell sculpted by Donatello rings sweetly in the colorful gardens, and, even now, Botticelli is working on a new altar piece. The Medici regard this as their private cloister. Lorenzo has summoned him to this post, and yet Savonarola has not even made a courtesy call on his famous patron. He is accountable to God and no other.

Savonarola, concluding the Mass, lifts his eyes to heaven before turning to the people for the benediction. He does not see the lovely Virgin or the bejeweled image of God, because his eyes focus on the scaffolding of the painter, Botticelli. Savonarola is willing to risk the scaffold of the hangman to purify the Church. Or, some might say, he chooses to ignore the beauty and love of God and to focus on his role as a martyr.

Tuesday

On Tuesday, January 2, 1492, there is no combat in Spain. This is a time for a formal surrender, a climactic celebration to the end of the war of *Santa Fe*, Holy Faith. The women of the court wear fine embroidered gowns, rivaled only by the elaborate robes of the clergy. The great cross of silver is carried and elevated by the Cardinal. Isabella, her yellow silk dress reflecting the sun, rides a donkey draped and harnessed in damask. She defers to her husband, but she is every inch a queen, in bearing, costume and influence. Fernando also rides a donkey, the symbol of peace and of triumph, which bore Jesus into Jerusalem on Palm Sunday and Roman generals in their victory parades.

Isabella of Castile and Fernando of Aragon had begun the unification of Spain with their marriage 22 years ago. Their teenage union has been blessed by children. Prince Juan is 13, and looking more manly each day. His younger sisters, Juana age 12, Maria age 9, and Catalina age 6, enjoy the public attention. Their 21 year old sister, Isabel, has changed from the black cloth of widowhood to a blue and gold brocade. For a year, all Spain had mourned Prince Alfonso, son and heir of John II of Portugal. Isabel has grieved too, not from a sense of duty, but for the love she had shared with her 15 year old groom for a few months before he was killed in a fall from his horse. Now her mourning has officially ended. Her mother the queen is 41, her father the king is 39; this victorious celebration heralds a new glory for Spain and the hope of new alliances for their children.

8

Parades and promenades feature the noble families of Spain, a mixture of Visigoths, Celts, Romans, Jews, Arabs and Berbers who have flourished in Iberia and intermarried after being baptized as Christians. The *santos*, carved wooden figures of the saints, have been repainted and dressed in fine silks and laces for this festive public parade. "Ring the bell! *Toqué usted la campaña*". The Moslem sultans are driven from Spain forever. Priests offer thanks; soldiers parade. Ring the bell!

The Alhambra, building and garden, Granada, Spain.
Photograph by Sara Whittier.

Queen Isabella and King Fernando formally take possession of the Alhambra, the pleasure-palace and fortress of the Moors. Boabdil stands, a defeated man. True, he has his life and some men. He surrenders the keys of the Alhambra to his conquerors and retreats down the hill, through Granada and the yellow valley leading to the Mediterranean Sea. The sultan leaves behind a palace that matches the Koran's description of paradise: courtyards, lacy arches, gardens, and fountains. Waters from the Sierra Nevada Mountains sparkle as they flow through rivulets to spout from lions' mouths, splash in reflecting pools, shower out from fountains and, finally, gently water the rose, the myrtle and the orange trees. He will remain in a mountain retreat and pay tribute, the final ruler after 700 years of Moslem occupation in Spain.

Eight centuries earlier the Moors, wielding their sharp swords and securely seated on their stirrupped horses, had overrun the Iberian peninsula. Only in southern France were they stopped in their northward sweep, by Charles Martel in 732. These had been the Berbers, zealous converts to Islam. Arab sultans had replaced them and ruled as Caliphs of Toledo, Cordoba and Granada. Then gradually over the next 750 years, the Moors were pushed back towards the south, to Granada and ultimately North Africa.

The Alhambra had first been a towered fort on the steep hills above Granada. When the Arab Sultan, Mohammed al-Ahmar "the Red", took Granada in 1238 he began building the palace within the walls. His family had ruled to this day. Now this was the last Moorish stronghold.

Some rulers had been cruel, one inviting and then murdering thirty-six of the young men of a noble Christian family of Granada. Kidnapped señoritas were locked in its towers. Yet, poetry, medicine and the sciences flourished.

These Islamic rulers permitted more freedom to the Jews than had the barbaric and suspicious Visigoth Christians. Not only had philosophy and medicine flourished, but the knowledge of geography grew out of the intellectual climate of Moorish Spain.

The surrender of the Alhambra was the culmination of a 35 year attempt to bring Granada under Spanish rule. This fertile area stretching from Jaen to Malaga paid tribute to Castile in 1457, then stopped paying nine years later. The self-indulgent Enrique IV did nothing, but Fernando demanded payment in 1474. Ali-abu-al Hasan replied by attacking Zahara in 1481 and enslaving its citizens, who were sold as slaves in Granada. The Spanish women brought high prices, for they were graceful, beautiful, with shiny brown hair and white teeth.

In the middle of this epic power struggle, Ali fell in love with one of these beautiful slave women. His scorned wife was furious and got his people to depose him and install their son as Sultan. The son, Boabdil, paid tribute to Fernando for a while, and then refused. His father fled to Malaga, and his uncle attempted to control Granada.

Fernando was the victor over this divided trio. He sent 30,000 troops to destroy farms and vineyards and groves in order to complete a successful siege. Boabdil's appeal for help from the powerful Moslem world was fruitless. Still he received rather humane terms of surrender. Moors wishing to leave were given free passage to North Africa. Those remaining could keep their property, religion, laws and magistrates, and not pay any taxes for three years. Thereafter the usual rate, one-seventh of the crops, would go to Fernando and Isabella. Boabdil, known as Mohammed XI in the Arab world, was "the last of the Moors" to the Spanish.

One man joining the ranks of the triumphant troops of Aragon and Castile has more on his mind than this splendid victory over the Moors. Cristóbal Colón will plead again for support for his Enterprise of the Indies. The fervor of "los reyes catolicos[2]", is sincere. Ring the bell! The true faith will abide in all of Castile and Aragon. Ring the bell! Let the infidel bow down and surrender. Ring the bell! The tocsin from the Alhambra sounds not an alarm but proclaims independence to Granada and to all of Spain.

Cristóbal Colón is forty-one years old. He has offered his plan to Portugal and then to Spain over many years. He has felt frustrated, discouraged and old, and considered returning to Lisbon to eke out a living as a chart maker. But his charts show such promise! Eleven years ago, he had corresponded with Paolo del Pozzo Toscanelli of Florence. Cristóbal knew the short route west to Cipangu, Japan; he had Toscanelli's chart and had studied it and carried it these ten years. Hadn't he seen with his own eyes the body of an Indian washed ashore in the freezing waters of Greenland?

Cristóbal has sailed; he knows ships and wind and reckoning. He loves God and wants to carry the cross of Jesus Christ to the pagans. He has read and reread Marco Polo's accounts of Cathay and Cipangu, China and Japan. Surely, after the great victory over the Moors, the Spanish monarchs will underwrite his explorations.

Cristóbal Colón has his hearing at the Alhambra. He is refused support, again.

Monday

Germany's most famous artist, Albrecht Dürer, is in the middle of the journeyman phase of his education. For two years, since he completed his apprenticeship to painter Michael Wohlgemut in Nuremberg, Albrecht has been traveling and expanding his knowledge and skills. In two more years, he will return to Nuremberg and to a marriage arranged by his parents.

Arriving in Colmar, he first stops at the cathedral. Martin Schongauer's altarpiece Virgin of the Rosehedge is a revelation to the young painter. Wohlgemut had taught him to use oil paint. Dürer's 1490 portrait of his father shows a face with some wrinkles, a trace of stubble, framed by hair and clothing of distinctive textures, but Schongauer has included finer details of nature and landscape in his work. His Virgin sits among roses and cruel thorns. The setting and her face show her joy with the infant, mingled with the knowledge that this Christ Child will give himself for others.

Albrecht also knows of Schongauer's fine engravings and is glad to be in Colmar to work with him. As the son of a goldsmith, Albrecht has a talent and love for fine metal work. Martin Schongauer's engravings capture some of the depth of feeling and fine detail of this magnificent altarpiece. Dürer noticed that he signed his engravings, a new practice which the young man plans to emulate.

Young Dürer, a tall, sandy-haired twenty-year-old, finds himself knocking at the door of the Schongauer home and shop. "I'm Albrecht Dürer, journeyman artist from Nuremberg. I would like to meet Herr Schongauer."

13

"Come in, please. Sit down," welcomes the matronly woman. Certainly she hadn't modeled for the Virgin. "I'll find Herr Schongauer."

Albrecht rests his traveling sack on the floor by the wooden chair, but soon he is on his feet again as the woman returns from the shop followed by a man in a working smock. "Good day," he says.

"I'm Albrecht Dürer of Nuremberg, and I am pleased to meet the esteemed Martin Schongauer."

"I'm afraid you are mistaken. Martin died this last year."

Dürer sinks back into the chair, feeling more despair that his plans should be marred than real sorrow that the Master has died. "I didn't know. I'm sorry."

Martin's three brothers in Colmar are sympathetic to the young journeyman. Dürer is invited to stay, help in the shop, study the works of the Master and use his tools.

Tuesday

As Leonardo da Vinci emerges from the Sforza castle in Milan, he pauses before going to the stables for a horse. His patrons, Ludovico and Gian Galeazzo Sforza, command and servants appear with horse and outriders. At least Ludovico always gets this treatment. Nicknamed Il Moro because of the bush on his coat of arms, Ludovico rules Lombardy with Milan at its center. His young nephew, Gian, the rightful Duke of Milan, had been relocated to Pavia, and Leonardo had spent six months there, reading, designing for the cathedral, and painting. The demanding Il Moro had summoned him back to plan his wedding.

Leonardo had come from Florence ten years ago, after writing to the Sforzas of his skills in armaments, machines of war, sculpture and painting. The armaments had not only strengthened Ludovico's position, but had become an item of trade. The equestrian statue of Francesco, first of the ruling Sforzas and father of Ludovico and grandfather of Gian Galeazzo, is still a work in progress. The artist's meager pay can not finance the bronze for a huge horse and rider, although the model is almost completed and the plans for casting are drawn. Il Moro finds materials and labor to build this fortress-castle, but bronze goes to cannons and covered chariots. Although the castle is not completed, it is habitable, and Leonardo has his quarters there.

His horse is saddled when he arrives at the stable. The artist dresses more elegantly than the ruler; his shirt of braided ribbons is partially covered by his flowing cape of red wool, embroidered with purple silk. His felt hat is

15

topped by a jaunty plume. No doubt the grooms recognize him from a distance.

When Leonardo first came to do "the Horse", as the equestrian statue was called, he spent days at the stables sketching and observing. Four years ago, the plague had killed all the older stablehands, as well as 50,000 Milanese. The young grooms catch his eye. Always attracted to boys, Leonardo has threatened to replace Jachomo, his twelve-year-old companion who steals and lies and spills the wine, just to irritate him. The grooms are polite and helpful, but not as witty and unpredictable as Jachomo.

From the castle to the cathedral is a ten minute ride. For the wedding, Leonardo had draped the buildings in rich fabrics and arranged a procession of trumpeters and mounted guards. He designed a suit of gold for the Duke of Milan, which highlighted his fair complexion. He is not handsome but rules the richest area in Europe, and he is impressive. How Leonardo wishes that Ludovico had acted to implement his design for Milan. After the plague had run its course, Leonardo designed a city with two levels to raise pedestrians above the animals and delivery carts, but it wasn't built. Instead the imagination and resources of two men in their 40th year, Leonardo and Ludovico, were used to impress the teenage bride, Beatrice d'Este of Ferrara. Of course he must paint a portrait of this lovely and lively fifteen year old.

As the artist continues his ride, he sees the remnants of the great pageant he staged a few days ago. The grunts of the jousters, the music of the minnesingers and the shouts of the crowds only echo in his mind as the city returns to the hum of every day life. As if to justify the extravagance and to make this political alliance stronger, Ludovico arranged for his bride's brother, Alfonso, to marry Anna Sforza, Ludovico's niece. A double wedding is Il Moro's idea of efficient action. The cathedral was certainly large enough.

The airy lightness of hundreds of statues rising on pinnacles from the walls and buttresses of this massive cathedral never ceases to amaze Leonardo. He has walked on the roof mid that forest of saints, and drawn his plans for the completion of the dome. As a young apprentice, he had seen his master, Verrocchio, put the gilded sphere at the top of the imposing dome of the Florence's cathedral. Milan's cathedral-in-progress needs a lighter look.

Leonardo needs time to dream, and think, and analyze, and design. Observations recorded in his notebooks help him to focus the many ideas and subjects that attract him. His patron expects him to build a castle, complete a cathedral, paint his bride's portrait, plan a wedding, and finish the horse. Il Moro complains that his artist "never finishes anything". Leonardo decides to complete the model for the bronze of Francesco on his horse. At twice life-size, it could be a focal point for future festivities when Beatrice d'Este gives birth to a legitimate heir for the Sforza dynasty.

7th day of the 12th month, Year of the Pig

155 Ashikaga Dynasty, 4189

Sesshū, the Leonardo of Japanese painters, lives quietly in the country near Choshu. Of course he and Leonardo da Vinci knew nothing of each other, but both were honored and sought after in 1492, and revered after death. Sesshū evokes trees, rocks, mountains, and water with lines and washes so subtle that it appears he had flung ink on the paper in a burst of creative power. At times, he will use a bunch of straw as a brush. One more scroll by Sesshū has survived to 1992 because years ago its owner cut open his own body to give it protection from a fire.

"Ship of Snow" is the meaning of the name Sesshū. As a youth he drew beautifully. Now, at age 72 he is happy that he has chosen the life of a Zen Buddhist priest. Finding beauty in the commonplace is more appealing than traveling to new or exotic vistas. As a younger man, Sesshū went to China. The Chinese, at first politely and then more insistently, presented him with paper after paper, begging for a picture or even a line from the master's hand. Ming porcelains outshine Japanese efforts, but for painting there is only one Sesshū.

Here in Choshu the landscape is molded by the snow falls and lit by the pale angular rays of the January sun. Sesshū captures those subtle variations and timeless emotions.

The old man has a young visitor today. At fifteen Kanō Motonobu is already an artist. The gift of expression through drawing appears at a young age in every culture.

18

Sesshū looks for many minutes at the cranes which Kanō has painted. He smiles at the young man and again sends his eyes over the three pictures, noting how angles and lines, varying in width and intensity, combine to bring a reality, the essence of crane. He asks Kanō how he is able to record their precarious but graceful stance so completely. Kanō, energized by this praise, makes a soft crane call in his throat, rises from the mat where he has been sitting, and assumes the one-legged stance of a crane. Sesshū marvels that Kanō's knees don't bend backward, so convincing is the effect. It's really rather comical, but the wise old Sesshū doesn't laugh.

"Kanō Motonobu, I thank you for giving me two new ways to appreciate the crane, and I thank you for visiting me."

Sesshū reflects on this delightful meeting. Perhaps he should paint cranes. He ponders, "I know my cranes would be better for having met Kanō, but why should I struggle to do what Kanō has mastered. Maybe I should paint this lovely blue and white porcelain vase. These Chinese porcelains compare to our humble plates and cups as their silk does to our homespun wool." His fingers stroke the smooth surface of his Ming vase. With his eyes closed, the aging monk is surprised that words of comparison have added to his appreciation and knowledge, but his Zen disciplines make him question its reality. He longs for a larger awareness. It's time to meditate and free the soul to know.

February

Thursday

King Henry publishes a grant to Elizabeth, the queen consort, his mother-in-law.[3]

> *As it is the King's intention*
> *to invade France shortly in person,*
> *and the premises are insufficient*
> *to maintain the queen's dignity,*
> *the King therefore grants to her for life*
> *over and above the said premises for her dower,*
> *Pymperne, forests of Exmore.*

Henry isn't the only member of the English court to plan a trip to France. Bartolome Columbus realizes that Henry will finance his own ships, but none for Christopher. Bartolome has asked Christopher to join him in France to persuade King Charles to finance them.

13th day of the 12th month, Year of the Pig
155 Ashikaga Dynasty, 4189

Awata's[4] wife prepares tea for him with politeness and grace. When the water is boiling heartily above a fire of twigs, she kneels to pour it over the tea leaves waiting in a bowl. She adds a pinch of salt, waits for the leaves to settle to the bottom and then offers the bowl to her husband. First Awata drinks, then she in turn sips from the same bowl. The Zen Buddhist monk's practice of drinking from the same bowl was now a part of the Japanese tea ceremony.

Bowing to his wife, Awata leaves his home to walk to the office where he serves as an appointee of Shogun Yoshitane. Awata used to enjoy representing the century old Ashikaga dynasty, particularly his service to the old Shogun Yoshimata who built the Silver Pavilion to support arts and drama. The past few years, since Yoshimata's death, have brought more frequent unrest and challenges to the traditional feudal system. Ikkoikki, uprisings of the Ikko, is what these insurrections are being called by Awata's office. The Ikko are also called the Pure-Land Sect and foment their revolution in Buddhist monasteries, even attacking rival monasteries which do not subscribe to their land reform agenda. Awata wishes those monks would attend to their prayers and meditations; he decides to delay his arrival at the office.

Kyoto offers many diversions, and his favorite is the Tea House of the New Moon. The courtesans there not only sing beautifully and dance like iris bending to a wind, but they still serve tea in the old way. Tea has long ago

22

left the realm of medicine and become a ritual of polite amusement. The nuances of boiling water have been celebrated in poetry. Some think it is perfect for the infusion when tiny bubbles appear at the edge of the pot. AWATA believes the water should be removed from the fire as the first round bubbles appear in the center. The attentive courtesan sees to that detail, and makes him feel included. He prefers these refinements to the robust boil his wife uses.

The courtesan in her silk kimono with lowered eyes separates the tea leaves, blossoms and stems, and selects a combination to suit the occasion. Would AWATA like the strength of a bull, a soothing healing brew, or one that will open his heart to the poetry and beauty around him? The young pekoe leaves with a look of white down are a mainstay. Using a little mortar and pestle, the courtesan powders the leaves he has selected. Just as the water starts to steam she removes it from the fire and adds the powdered leaves but no salt. Kneeling before AWATA, she uses a bamboo whisk to stir the mixture and remove the tiny particles of tea.

She pours his tea into a cup. AWATA returns her bow as he accepts not just a cup of tea but a bit of steaming history, some poetry in a cup.

Thursday

The greatest lyric poet of medieval India, Kabir, still plies his trade of weaving. His poetic songs look for beauty in the everyday.

Put imagination away, stand fast in that which you are.

Perhaps the influence of his Mohammedan father is reflected in that thought. Kabir's mother was Hindu, a Brahman maiden who became fascinated with Moslem preaching and her husband. Kabir also wrote,

Real is in your home.

One day 1,500 people gather in Benares on the banks of the Ganges to meditate. Kabir is invited to read his poems and he accepts. He is a venerable aged man, some say he is 96 years of age, others that he is 52. In any case, he will live 25 more years, and when Mohammedan and Hindu leaders both lay claim to his body, it turns to flowers.

Before reading his poems to the assembled crowd, Kabir quietly asks for his fellow poet Mirabai. He suspects that she has not been invited because she is female, for her poems are wonderful. Finding that she was omitted, he refuses to read unless she is included. He waits for two days, and Mirabai is included.

Kabir's poems explore the world of the senses and the individual response. He asks the meditators to consider,

Live justly

and certainly his actions make his words as real as your home.

Tuesday

Nuremberg is the home of Barbara Dürer. The two Albrecht Dürers, her husband and son, are traveling. The journeyman phase of her son's art education is in mid-stream; three cities in two years, all less than 200 miles from Nuremberg. Barbara receives and saves a letter from her husband. Albrecht Dürer Sr.'s visit to the court of Saxony has been a success; he has been appointed Goldsmith to Frederick III.

Barbara stays home with her younger son; two sons are the only children to survive infancy. Married at fifteen, she has given birth to seventeen children.[5] Hard work, prayer, few possessions, and frequent visits to church are her routine. Three marvelous churches adorned with sculpture grace Nuremberg. The Sebalduskirche, nearing the end of its third major remodel in 100 years, has its western tower almost complete and glowing stained glass windows in process.

The winding, unpaved streets lead past sturdy and comfortable houses. The Dürers' house is small but tidy, in spite of the meat being cooked over an open fire on a spit in the house. Sleeping quarters are upstairs. The sloping roof points down to the narrow street.

Nuremberg attracts scholars, artists, and businessmen. It is a free city, governed by a city council of 34 men since 1348. The city has stood on the banks of the Pegnitz River for 500 years. Dürer neighbors include Regiomontanus, an astronomer and classical scholar, and Peter Henlein, one of many clockmakers. Peter had been making spring wound clocks for twenty years, although

25

many people still prefer the weights and gears of the earlier design. Now, he is experimenting with a small portable clock, the first watch.

Much of the business centers around metals: wire, needles, pins, and weapons, including the matchlock pistol. Tin and iron are the basis for all kinds of vessels and machinery. Leather bellows are hand powered to heat the fire under the metals. The water wheel provides power, about 10 horsepower, to draw wire. The wealthy families of Nuremberg invest in mining.

The making of paper is becoming mechanized, and printing has flourished in the forty years since Johannes Gutenberg, a goldsmith of Mainz on the Rhine had first assembled moveable type to print the Bible. Nuremberg scholars are completing a marvelous volume — *The World Chronicle*, a history from creation to the present.

Albrecht Dürer is bound for another bookmaking center. He left Colmar with a gift of several engravings from Martin Schongauer's brothers, a letter of recommendation to their brother in Basel, some bread and cheese for the journey, and a small payment for his help in their shop. Young Dürer showed such promise with engraving and wood block carving, that they felt sure that their brother in Basel could connect his talents with the book printing industry there.

The broad valley of the Rhine River links Colmar and Basel. No longer is the river a boundary between the Roman Empire and the Germanic tribes. The Romans are gone, and the Goths have built Gothic cathedrals. Dürer can use his pay to book passage on a trading boat on the Rhine, or perhaps a captain will exchange passage for a watercolor of the wide river, or the Black Forest on the left. Dürer goes south to Basel, further from Nuremberg, but with dreams of going to Florence and to Antwerp, which he will realize one day.

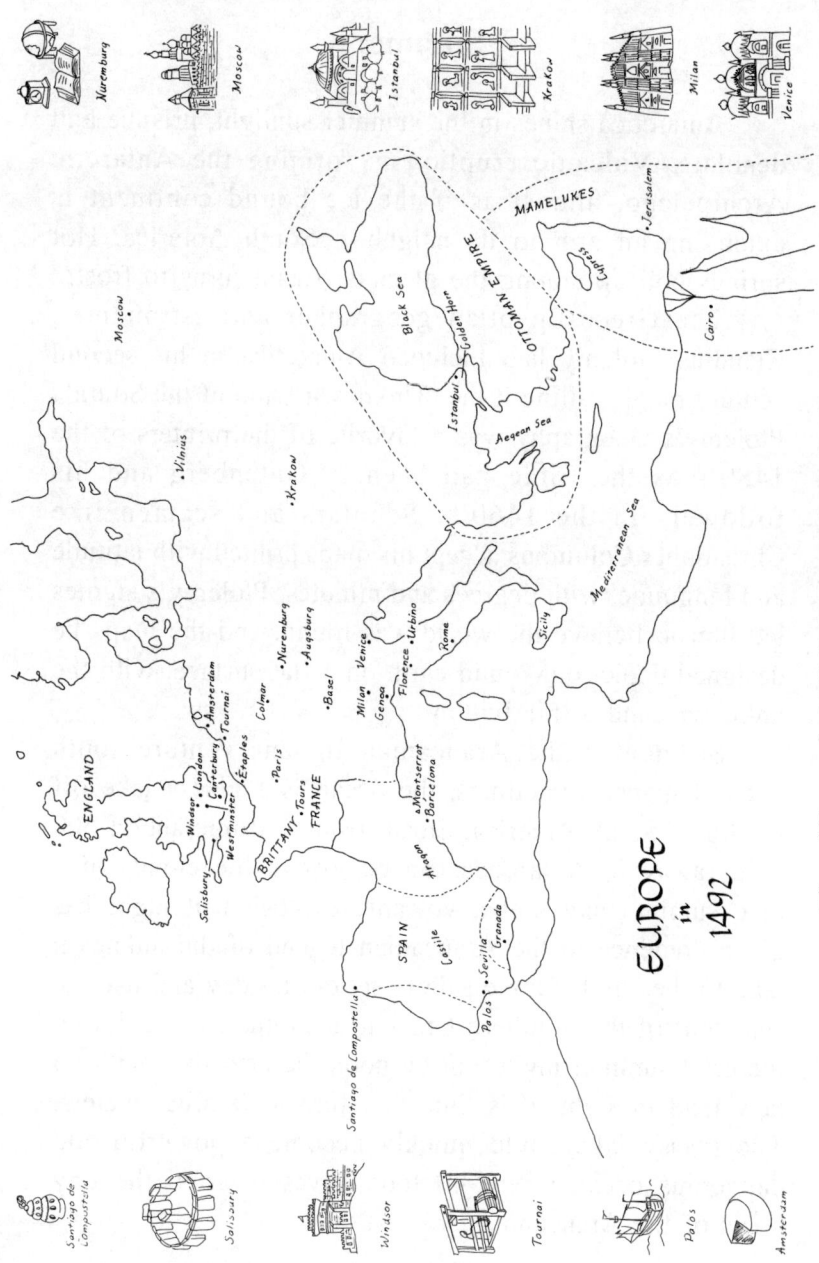

Map of Europe in 1492 by Barbara M. Garlinghouse.

Summer

Antarctica shines in the summer sunlight, pristine and desolate. Volcanic eruption is forming the Antarctic Archipelago, almost as if the ice bound continent is extending an arm to its neighbor, South America. Hot springs boil up among the glaciers; steam turns to frost.

The Greco-Egyptian geographer and astronomer, Claudius Ptolemy had included Antarctica in his second century maps, calling it the "Unknown Land of the South". Ptolemy's Geography was a favorite of the printers of the 1480's as the Bible had been to Gutenberg and his followers in the 1460's. Scholars and seamen like Christopher Columbus accept his maps printed with latitude and longitude, with degrees and minutes. Ptolemy's studies led him to believe the world was round, and the maps he designed depict our round earth on a flat surface, with the unknown land at the bottom.

Seamen of the Araucanian Indians venture south without maps. Sometimes, the ocean is a glassy lake off the tip of South America. Steam from volcanic action 600 miles away in Antarctica can be lost in the clouds of a blue summer sky, but a volcanic explosion at night has given credence to the Araucanian legend of the unknown land to the south. Brave sailors set out by day and use the star light of the Southern Cross to continue sailing during the brief summer night, but by noon the next day, with no new land in sight, it is time to return to familiar waters. The glassy lake could quickly become a powerful and dangerous ocean where 40 foot waves dwarfed the tiny boats of the Araucanians.

Across the strait, the grey rocky shoreline dotted with summer grasses provides a home for seventeen different species of penguins. These flightless birds excel in swimming in the cool arctic waters, feeding on krill and small fishes. Their crowded rookeries on the rocky shoreline and the floating icebergs offer them ample protection from their predators in the ocean. Father penguins have gone without eating to guard their eggs for two long winter months. Then the mothers take over feeding the hatchlings with regurgitated krill. Now young penguins are nearing independence, not only in the Antarctic, but on the islands off the west coast of South America that are cooled by Antarctic currents. These charming animals, so striking in their black and white feathers, have a comical waddle on land where they are virtually defenseless.

The Araucanians, and the Incas to their north, kill thousands of them in a day with nets and stone knives. The loyal parents guarding their downy chicks offer little resistance. Emperor penguins and the smaller gentoo and chin-strap penguins are killed for their meat and their leather. The penguin hides are transported home and made into purses, slippers and clothing. The Inca ruler, Huayna Cápac, enjoys this luxurious leather. The guano is collected for fertilizer. It looks like red tile where it paves the rookery. The orange krill in the penguin's diet gives this color. To get fresh eggs with bright red yolks, the sailor-hunters will return in November.

The Incas load the penguin products into their boats and begin the journey from the Antarctic seas to the 10,000 foot elevations near the equator. The Incas are well organized as these expeditions show. With their roads and runners along the Andes foothills, their influence extends throughout the continent's Pacific coast.

1st day of the 1st month, Year of the Rat

124 Ming Dynasty, 4190

All of Canton is celebrating the new year. It's a time for feasting, dramas, and parades. Everyone takes a holiday from work, except the astrologers. The year of the Pig has ended. The year of the Rat marks not only a new year but a return to the beginning of the twelve year cycle of the Chinese calendar.[6] Diviners are being asked advice for the next twelve years. Chinese astrologers observe the faintest of distant stars for omens but lack the mathematics to be astronomers.

Farm families are crowding into the city for the celebration. The rich delta of the Canton River and the warm tropical climate make it possible for them to grow three rice crops a year, as well as tea and sugar cane. The narrow city streets echo with the sounds of firecrackers. Boys and girls from the country dash into doorways and between columns to make room for the dragon dancers. The huge dragon head of papier-mâché is painted brightly and jingles with bells. The men beneath it are average height, about five feet tall, but they use poles to manipulate their giant puppet. The 30 foot long body of red silk with fringe covers more men and boys who use their poles to make the dragon twist and turn, rise and fall, with great energy.

Some of the houseboats have come from nearby canals to dock at the north bank of the Canton River. These boats are homes, combined with offices, workshops and stores. The cloisonne craftsman can make a beautiful vase. He

30

bends and fires the bronze cloisons which hold thick enamel paint in lovely patterns. After the final polishing, the craftsman can sell it from his boat. His shop, store, wife and children occupy the same boat. Food, firewood, even a doctor are available in neighboring boats. Cantonese are born and die on houseboats and can live a full life without setting foot on land. Still, most enjoy the streets and squares of the city, especially on a holiday.

The wealthy women of Canton avoid the bustling streets this evening. Their tiny feet are considered a mark of breeding and beauty but are a handicap in crowds. Their silk dresses have a gentle swaying motion because these ladies have been subjected to foot binding throughout their childhood. Their mincing steps delight their husbands, and they have servants to wait on them.

Wealthy merchant families celebrate a White Feast for the new year. Everyone dresses in white as a symbol of good luck. Pictures of protective spirits are attached to doors. This custom started more than a thousand years ago when a T'ang emperor heard demons in his bedroom. He couldn't sleep until his ministers sat up all night to guard him. Eventually he had an artist paint portraits of Ch'in and Hu, the vigilant ministers, on his door, and the emperor continued to feel protected. The family exchanges gifts: white cloth, a white horse, decorative pieces of ivory, white jade, silver and gold. Before and during the feast, steaming hot rice wine is served. It is laced with spices and drugs.

The revered grandfather of 80 remembers when the emperor lived in Nanking and his New Year's gifts were 81 white horses, piles of silks, and 81 pearls. Nine times nine is an auspicious number. His son remembers when all men were forced to provide free labor to build and repair roads and canals and even to erect buildings. The new emperor has moved north to Beijing and now, for the third year, taxes are settled, as are most other transactions, with paper money, and canal builders get paid. All debts must be settled for the new year, so some families feel very wealthy.

The 80-year-old continues to reminisce, "For more than a thousand years we have traded with the people to the west. When I was a young man, our emperor sent his eunuchs as ambassadors as far as the Straits of Hormuz. From Aden to Malay, states paid tribute to our emperor. Cheng Ho was a brave admiral and made seven voyages west. When I was 20, he returned from his final voyage bringing tribute from Mecca and ten other states."

The white-robed family and guests still think of Canton, with more than a million people, as the hub of the world, trading porcelains and lacquer ware to the ships that come up the river from the South China Sea. But they are more isolated now than they were 200 years ago, because the Mohammedan Arabs are gaining more and more power.

The dragon dancers have reached the gateway of the largest Buddhist temple. The slender columns leave ample room for the dragon dancers to please the crowd. The crowd laughs as a young boy takes refuge behind his father's legs when the dragon snorts smoke from its nostrils. The gateway faces the river; some houseboats have a prime location to appreciate the three-tiered tiled roof with all corners turned up to heaven. But to appreciate how the slender columns can support a massive roof so that it seems to float, one must come on land. A system of bracket-arm sets with complex mortise-and-tenon joints supports the roof and please the eye. Looking from below, the cloisonne craftsman sees a graduated series of bracket-arms, decorated with flowers and patterns in red, green and blue paint. The beauty of the complex geometric patterns appeals to his sense of design. The functional strength has been proven and established. The gateway design comes from *Building Standards*, a book of more than 1000 pages that has been the definitive source for Chinese architects and builders for 300 years. The book, printed from wood blocks on paper, required that temples and government buildings be set on a north-south axis with the gateway to the south. This allowed for winter sunlight and summer shade; today the weather is mild, but summer can bring 90 degree weather. As worshippers approach the central bay of the temple, they face north, and north is the direction of superiority.

Buddhism is but one of China's religions. For more than 2000 years Tao, the Heavenly Way, taught by Lao-tze has offered peace through the unity of Yang and Yin, man and woman, lord and servant, heaven and earth. Confucians worship great men, ancestors, and "T'ien". "T'ien" could be the god of heaven or the forces of justice and goodness. Fears and beliefs in spirits, in trees, snakes, or the wind persist, especially among the farming peoples. When Buddhist monks came from India 1500 years ago, many Chinese accepted the teachings of Siddharta Guatama. Six hundred fifty years later a group of Nestorian Christians was received and given protection, but later the Cantonese expelled them. Still later, Coptic Christians from Baghdad built churches and Roman Catholic missionaries following Marco Polo had 5,000 converts in 1307. Persian Jews have been settled in K'ai-feng for 330 years and freely worship at their synagogue.

Most Chinese are drawn to mysticism and are open-minded on all religions, even Islam, but Islam is a political and economic threat. For this is the new year 124 of the Ming Dynasty. The trade and tribute that have poured into Canton for 1300 years are waning. Rats are admired

33

for their persistence and ability to flourish by adapting to new situations. The Chinese unite to honor their emperor, pray for personal success and happiness, and launch the Year of the Rat with firecrackers and skyrockets.

8th day of Dhu'l Hijja, 896 A.H.[7]

ABDUL and KHALID wake with the first rays of the sun. The palm trees flourishing by the oasis provide dates to eat but little shade. These worshippers of Allah have traveled four days from Medina. Today, if it is Allah's will, they will be in Mecca for the Hajj.

All followers of Islam must make a pilgrimage to the holy city once in their lifetime. Often it is the culmination of a pious life: prayer five times a day, charity for the poor, living justly with other men, and fasting at Ramadan. ABDUL and KHALID are brothers in their 20's. Their father made his Hajj three years ago. Hajj is always between the 8th and 15th day of the twelfth month. Father had appreciated the cooler days, for Hajj in 893 A.H. had corresponded to January 26, 1489 A.D. He encouraged his sons to journey on this holy mission while they were still young and before Hajj moved into the long days of burning sunlight.

Sometimes the camels traveled in the evening. Although the moon was still a crescent, as the Arab travelers neared Mecca, fires were lit to guide the worshippers.

KHALID took the camels to the spring while ABDUL packed their tent and belongings. Although their family was well known in Medina, this day they dressed in simple white gowns. All Moslem men are of equal value to God, and those participating in the Hajj put aside all position and pride.

Riding south on their camels, their heads covered to protect them from the sun, each man was left to his own

35

thoughts. Soon the road south to Mecca became crowded with pilgrims. Many had come from Jeddah. That port on the Red Sea was an entrance for Islamic worshippers from North Africa and Istanbul. Some had left Granada wondering why Allah and their fellow believers had not come to help them against Fernando. Most were walking.

All the faithful stopped for prayers, facing and bowing toward Mecca. At the conclusion, KHALID said to his older brother, "ABDUL, there are some men here older than our father who look too frail to walk to Mecca. Would it be a good act, pleasing to God, if we let them ride our camels?"

"KHALID, God has shown you this path," ABDUL replied, "I will offer my camel, too."

The brothers soon found that their Bedouin dialect was not easily understood. Their offers of help were received with polite but incredulous looks. Gestures quickly resolved the dilemma, and soon a grateful, elderly worshipper was resting his weary feet on each camel.

The bells on the camel harnesses jingle merrily as the brothers lead their ships of the desert. Now the brothers can talk, and ABDUL, the elder, feels obligated to make sure his younger brother is fully briefed for the days ahead.

"When we get to Mecca, we will enter the Great Mosque. In the central courtyard is the Kaaba, a temple built by Abraham to worship the one and only God. We must walk seven times around the Kaaba. Abraham chose this spot to tell his first son, Ishmael, of God, because it had an ancient holy stone, that is still in the Kaaba."

"But Abraham built the Kaaba thousands of years ago, before Moses and Jesus. How old is this ancient stone?"

"It is from the garden of Adam and Eve, the first people. The 'people of the book' tell of Eden; Eden is here. But the tribes of Arabia forgot the God of Abraham, and filled the Kaaba with their idols. 900 years ago, God sent the archangel Gabriel to Mohammed, and told him to preach against the idol worship at the Kaaba."

"So, now we go to worship the one God where Abraham, Ishmael and Haggar did."

"We can," replies ABDUL, "but Mohammed had many battles before he convinced the people of Mecca. But the Koran, God's word and the prophetic sayings and..."

"I see the Minarets of Mecca," KHALID interrupts. "There is no god but God, and Mohammed is His prophet."

ABDUL is silent for a moment as his eyes identify the graceful prayer towers appearing in the wavy refraction of the desert horizon. The camel bells continue to jingle, and the pace of the pilgrims accelerates ever so slightly.

The younger brother muses, "Perhaps in Mecca we shall see God in the holy Kaaba. One thing is sure, God always sees us."

March

10th-11th days of the 1st month, Year of the Rat 124 Ming Dynasty, 4190

FANG LE has traveled ten days from the south to Beijing. It is the trading capital of northern China as well as the Emperor's Capital City. FANG had hoped to arrive by mid-day, but the long distance over dusty roads delayed him. FANG is happy the moonlight and lantern lights guide him to the Tung-ah gate. His horses are loaded with raw elephant ivory. He stops at the first Inn he sees, and asks the innkeeper for a discount since he is arriving so late.

"No, no discount. You are lucky we have a bed for you, and a place for your horses."

FANG LE is getting short of money but is too tired to argue. He pays the full amount. In the morning, he will start selling his ivory to the carvers.

The annual Lantern Bazaar fills an area one mile by one-half mile near the Tung-ah gate, the gate of Eastern Peace. For nine days, an auspicious number, the Bazaar operates day and night, with colorful lanterns to illuminate the darkness. Nobles, eunuchs, great merchants, small merchants and craftsmen come to buy and sell jade, porcelain, bronzes, silk, cinnabar lacquerware, incense, ivory and more. Regular trading takes place three times a month; three-quarters of all the craftsmen of China are registered in Beijing: 180,000 of them. This is not a regular trade day, but an annual event that attracts merchants from great distances.

Beijing has been transformed from a military garrison to a cosmopolitan city by the Ming Emperors. The walls and nine gates are vestiges of its military beginnings. The

Great Wall to the north is being strengthened, and moving the capital here has given security from the Mongols. Although they ruled from Genghis Khan to Kublai Khan, they have been driven north by the Mings. Emperor Yung-lo completed most of the imperial buildings 70 years ago. The city around them has continued to grow in size and in beauty.

Hung Chih was born in a small palace in the west section. As Emperor, his home is now at the center of the Forbidden City. It is a city as large as the Lantern Bazaar and includes great halls as well as his personal living quarters. Hung Chih seldom appears in public. The best of China comes to him in the Forbidden City. Musicians playing zithers and flutes soothe him. Drama troops entertain, using a roofed gateway for a stage. Hung Chih is a quiet man who loves extravagant and unusual things. He and his ministers have arranged for him to have his privacy and to increase his wealth.

The Emperor owns official fields, and his viceroy orders people to plant the mulberry and jujube seedlings he distributes. The crop is the Emperor's, and the cost of the seedlings is returned, multiplied by 1000. Some of his subjects had avoided taxes by registering as "imperial land grants", but Hung Chih has stopped this abuse. Over the years, taxes have been paid as 30,000 cotton uniforms, or 400,000 pieces of porcelain, or 30 million piculs of grain.[8] Although the Chinese have used paper money for 1000 years, Hung Chih has just begun collecting taxes in that manner and in silver. He needs 8 million piculs of rice, wheat and barley just to supply his court and troops in Beijing for a year, and another 8 million for the frontier garrisons. His ministers can negotiate him a good price.

The palace guards, chosen for their six foot height and their loyalty, are extending their patrols during the

Lantern Bazaar. In the early morning light, they see two men asleep in bed rolls by the giant tortoise statue that guards the entrance to the tomb of Yung-lo. The sleepers' fire has burned down to a few embers. The soldiers have their guns ready as they approach shouting, "What are you doing here?"

Startled from sleep, LU JUNG replies, "We were sleeping, of course."

"Stand up, and no tricks!"

LU JUNG and his son see the guns and uniforms and quickly comply. The soldiers rip open one pack and find leather horse bridles with bronze bits. The gilded bronze decorations catch the faint morning light.

"What are you doing here?" the captain asks again.

LU JUNG bows, "We are merchants coming from the north to the Lantern Bazaar".

"You are on the marble road, where no ordinary man may travel. Pack up immediately and be gone. Your bazaar is still an hour's ride."

"My son and I beg your forgiveness," LU JUNG responds. "We will do as you say. Please take some bridles for your own use."

The palace guards put away their guns, and each grabs a bridle before riding to a hill where they can observe the intruders.

LU JUNG and his son move quickly. Their horses must be packed. LU speaks quietly, "My son, be careful, but as we leave, look around you. Beyond the tortoise are camels and lions and elephants of stone, as tall as two men. In the night, we must have stopped at the great Red Gate to the Ming tombs. The soldiers might have shot us as grave robbers."

41

12th day of the 1st month, Year of the Rat
124 Ming Dynasty, 4190

Emperor Hung Chih has received so many requests for audiences from the merchants at the Lantern Bazaar that he has decided that he wants to see for himself. His eunuchs protest that they will buy only the most beautiful lacquerware, the rarest jade, at the lowest prices for their Emperor. Hung Chih is wise enough to know that many will try to line their sleeves with his money. Yet, he will not go all the way to the Eastern Peace gate and mix with the crowds and dust.

Three main palaces and several smaller ones adjoin the Imperial gardens housing wives, concubines, ministers, eunuchs, and servants. Besides these 9,000 rooms, three great halls guarded by huge bronze lions or encircled by marble terraces, are filled with treasures and await the Emperor's ceremonial visits. He accepts his fabulous world as ordinary because it was largely completed before he was born. A high wall and moat offer security, but other rivers and canals within the Forbidden City are spanned by graceful marble bridges.

Selected merchants are invited to bring their best wares to Tien'anmen Gate. Hung Chih is carried from his palace past the great halls to the edge of the Forbidden City. The Emperor's palanquin is designed to coordinate with his unique marble staircases. With poles of the palanquin on their shoulders, the bearers walk on two parallel marble staircases; the Emperor rides between. Under his comfortable passenger carriage, friendly dragons

42

are sculpted in white marble. It is a special stairway for one who never needs to walk.

The merchants see their Emperor approach. All kneel, and at a sign from the main eunuch, they bow in unison, putting heads to the ground in the kow tow. The palanquin travels purposefully through Tien'anmen, the Gate of Heavenly Peace, and among the merchants. At a sign from the Emperor, his entourage stops. Hung Chih listens to some bronze bells; thirty of varying sizes would cover six repeats of the five toned scale. He leaves a minister to complete the purchase. Much of the porcelain is no different than what he already owns, not interesting. Lu Jung and his son haven't been invited to this gathering; horses and bridles, fruits and vegetables stay at the Lantern Bazaar. Fang Le is at Tien'anmen and hopes to sell his largest elephant tusk to the Emperor.

By chance, the Emperor spots the magnificent ivory. He sends Ma Wen-Sheng, his tax reformer, to strike a bargain. "Ming" means brilliant, and this Ming Emperor combines a brilliant mind with a love of decorative art. He will enjoy approving a pattern for this ivory and adding the brilliant finished piece to his city of treasures.

Tuesday, Michelangelo's Birthday

Michelangelo Bounarroti has found his art and his home. He is living in the palace of Lorenzo de Medici on the Via Larga in Florence and working on a sculpture in the gardens. There, surrounded by statues from ancient Greece and Rome, talented young sculptors flourish, encouraged by their generous patron. Lorenzo the Magnificent has provided Michelangelo with a room, an allowance, meals with the family and guests, and access to his library.

The wisdom and humor of the Greeks and Romans is being rediscovered in Lorenzo's library. Actually, it is Florence's library, as it is open to all citizens. Here, truly, was the first public library, although citizenship is limited to about 5,000 of the 20,000 residents of the city.

Papa Bounarroti had a title but no money and had beat young Michelangelo for wasting his time drawing. Just five years ago when Michelangelo was eleven, his father had relented and sent him to the studio of Ghirlandajo to learn to paint. Now, after showing much promise under Ghirlandajo, the lad was abandoning the paint brush for sculpture. Michelangelo could see the figures within the stone, and worked feverishly to free them. His *Battle of the Centaurs and Lapiths* was occupying him totally.

For one so young, he works with speed and sureness. The chisels are placed precisely; the chips come showering. This small relief carving is his second work to come down to us today. He had not yet proven himself to be entrusted with a giant block of marble for a David or a Moses. But his genius in portraying the human form in action is

44

evident. The Lapiths were a fun loving tribe in Greek mythology who planned a festive wedding celebration. They invited the Centaurs, jolly creatures with horses legs and human torsos. The wine flowed, the Centaurs imbibed, and the revelry got out of hand as a Centaur grabbed the bride and trotted off with her. The Lapiths rallied to rescue her, and the battle ensued. Michelangelo captures the turmoil of the struggling bodies in deep relief carving. By comparison, his earlier *Madonna of the Steps* seems as cool as the geometric steps behind her.

Lorenzo comes to the garden to invite his most talented sculptor to dinner. He hugs the young man, praises his work, and urges him to join him for dinner, for this day Michelangelo is seventeen. He appears even younger, weighing barely one hundred pounds and standing a bit more than five feet tall. He has almost reached his adult size, so small compared to the massive figures of the Sistine Chapel frescoes and the monumental sculptures for the tombs of Pope Julius and the Medici family that lay ahead along with a tremendously productive life to age eighty-nine. Lorenzo at age forty-three is ailing and more confined to his villa and garden. The greatest patron of the Italian Renaissance is nearing the end of his life as Michelangelo is beginning his career.

Tuesday

Before the fasting and abstinence of Lent, eat, drink and enjoy some fornication. Masks and capes hide all identities as the revelers parade and dance in the Piazza San Marco. Savory pork and spicy chicken give one a thirst for more Chianti. Carnival! Meat and flesh! As a boisterous group of celebrants nears the porches of San Marco, the pigeons scatter. They flutter past the 300 year old mosaics on this Byzantine cathedral, and a few alight on the gilded bronze horses on the porch above. These horses, taken from the hippodrome in Constantinople, in 1204, represent the preeminence of Venice as a sea power. It took the Ottoman Turks to conquer completely the Byzantines and change their Constantinople to Istanbul. By that time, the four horses had already left for Venice.

Who knows what these four life-sized horses have seen since they were created in the Greek world of 13 centuries ago? They face the large Piazza San Marco but might take a sidelong glance down the piazzetta between the bell tower and the Doge's palace. The celebration is even wilder in this location. A pair of young party-goers know their stomachs are rebelling, and dash toward the canal. It is bad luck to walk between the columns topped by St. Mark and St. Theodore, but the crowd and urgency are a more compelling reason. Good luck for one; he removes his black and white harlequin mask and vomits in the canal. Bad luck for the other. His costume and mask are finished for this Carnival.

A short gondola ride away the printer, Matteo de Parma is assembling the pages of *La Commedia*. The first

46

edition of Dante Alighieri's work was illustrated with wood block prints, each hand colored. The commentary by Cristoforo Landino may have helped men to understand the book Dante had written 150 years ago. Clearly Dante had found an audience. Matteo found a second edition offered a chance for quicker profits, so he is willing to work through Carnival.

Another update is in progress. Johannes Santretter is editing the *Astronomical Tables* of Alfonso the Wise of Spain. Originally built on the theories of Ptolemy for the Caliph of Cordoba about 400 years ago, they were revised around 1270 for Alfonso X. Once Santretter sets these figures on the motion of celestial bodies accurately in type, they will not suffer from errors by a copyist. The poetry of Dante has a wider appeal, but Ptolemy's, or Claudius Ptolemaeus, works in geography and astronomy have a growing audience. To think that a Greek who wrote 1350 years ago should be an important source on the heavens and the earth!

Saturday, the Druid New Year

JONATHAN WHITANNER of Salisbury delivers his fine white leather to the seamstress of the Earl of Salisbury. Would the Earl himself have a lovely embroidered vest, or the ladies have white kid gloves? Shyly he asks the seamstress what she will charge to make some gloves for his betrothed, MARGARET of Sarum. Their wedding plans have been announced, and although the ceremony will be simple, they are to be wed in Salisbury Cathedral. Its tall single spire has dominated the skyline of their valley of five rivers for more than 100 years.

The seamstress, though the day is foggy and cold, has a warm heart, and volunteers to make the gloves as her wedding gift, if she has enough time. "When is the wedding to be?"

"Not until April 23rd, the day after Easter," JONATHAN replies.

"Plenty of time, but are you sure that MARGARET will be the right wife for you?"

WHITANNER looks almost as white as his leather, although his many freckles and shaggy brown beard disguise his blanched appearance. He mumbles and waits for the gossipy seamstress to continue.

"Early this morning, the cook went to Stonehenge to celebrate the New Year, and reported that MARGARET of Sarum was there, dressed in white, blowing on a ram's horn and bowing toward the rising sun. Heathen practices, I'd say!"

The ancient mysterious circle of monoliths held a fascination for MARGARET. Could she be a serious Druid?

Was she just enjoying an early morning walk on the Salisbury Plain? JONATHAN thinks of how attractive she is, with her independent free spirit, and decides not to question her. How many others harbor some belief in sun worship? Their bans are being read in church each Sunday. Will she be publicly challenged as unfit to be a Christian wife? Probably not, and after they are married, she will be too busy with babies to put on a white robe and parade around at dawn to celebrate the Druid New Year.

Monday

Two great princes of the Italian Renaissance, Pope Innocent VIII and Lorenzo de Medici of Florence share more than the fact their deaths are imminent. They are bound by family ties. In their era of political power grabs, economic growth and shifting loyalties, loyalty to family first is a guiding principle.

Innocent VIII, born Giovanni Batista Cibó in Genoa, is 60 years old and has been Pope for eight years. Lorenzo at age 43, ailing from the gout that had killed his father and grandfather, has earned the title, the Magnificent, for his twenty-three year rule of Florence. His daughter, Maddelena, has married the Pope's son. Yes, this Pope acknowledges his two children, fathered in his youth, before he took a vow of chastity.

Today, these fathers-in-law are planning the future of Rome and continuing to cement their family ties. The Pope had appointed Giovanni de Medici, a Cardinal of the Catholic Church. Lorenzo boasted that his youngest son, at fourteen, was the youngest Cardinal "that has ever existed". At sixteen Giovanni is publicly joining the College of Cardinals in Rome.

Lorenzo's letter of March 12, 1492, gives his son, Giovanni, advice to be grateful to God, and to repay His gifts by a "pious, chaste, exemplary life". His advice extends to clothing, food, and dealing with people. It is not just advice for a student, but for a lifetime. In exactly 21 years, Giovanni was elected Pope, took the name Leo, then was ordained a priest, and eventually excommunicated Martin Luther.

50

KAROLVS · VIII · FRACIE · CISCILIE · AC · IHLEM · REX ·

Charles VII Introduced to the Redeemer by Mary Magdalene by Jean Baptiste Poyet, from his prayer book. Reproduced by courtesy of the Pierpont Morgan Library, New York, M. 50, f. 10v. Refer also to November 6, page 201.

Wednesday

The newlyweds are taking in the air and admiring the majestic river, the leafy trees, the stalks of asparagus punching through the earth. He is Charles VIII, age 21, King of France. She is Anne of Brittany, 15, his Queen. Her dowry is that part of France where Britons had so recently fought. With this marriage, perhaps the threats from Henry VII across the channel will subside.

Charles has been King since he was 13; just now he is beginning to rule. Another Anne, his sister, ten years older, has been an excellent regent. She has put down rebellions, mended fences, cut expenses and also taxes. After arranging this marriage, sister Anne has stepped into the background. Charles, seemingly secure from the English, is being courted by the Sforzas of Milan to join them in attacking Naples.

Traveling west this morning from Sully-Sur-Loire with the morning sun at their backs, the couple is beginning to appreciate their fine chateaux at Langeais where they were married. It had been a step into history to stay at Sully-Sur-Loire, a solid feudal fortress, guarding the crossing of the Loire River. They had slept in the upper floor apartment where a marvelous keel shaped wooden roof had stood without worms or rot or cobwebs since 1363. Those builders had used chestnut that had begun a curing process 100 years before construction.

Anne has been only slightly interested in the construction, but more in hearing the connection of the chateaux to Charles' grandfather, Charles VII and Joan of Arc. Grandfather had been living at Sully when Joan came

52

from a successful battle against the Earl of Shrewsbury to insist that Charles accompany her to Reims Cathedral to be anointed and crowned. All this happened before this young King was born, but his father told him the story often. To keep his bride amused, since she seems to tire of the landscape, Charles recites some history to the new Queen of France.

"*Grandpére* had been called 'king' since he was my age. He was married and had several children, but for seven years he was not crowned or anointed. So he was called the Dauphin and was harassed by the English who controlled Paris. Earlier in 1429, Joan, the maid of Orleans, was persuaded by her visions to come to my *grandpére* and convince him to be crowned. First, she came to Chinon, a medieval fort like Sully. We won't visit there as it's been neglected for years. But Joan's visit changed the course of the battles and French history, though before the final French victory, the English captured and burned her as a heretic in 1431."

Anne, her interest piqued, responds, "But she was a heretic, riding into battle in men's armor."

"Oh, no," Charles assures her, "the 1456 ecclesiastical court had declared the earlier verdict void. Besides, my father was six when Joan was ushered into the great hall at Chinon. Her claims as a messenger of God were known. She had fasted and prayed for two days. The clergy had pronounced her pious and a virgin, a suitable vessel for God's word. Nevertheless, the 27 year old Dauphin had a test of his own. He put others in royal robes in positions of honor and hid himself with the 300 people in the hall. Joan entered and went to him immediately, though she had never seen him before."

His grandson, Charles, thinks better of telling Anne the rest of that meeting. Joan had assured the Dauphin that he really was the rightful heir to the throne. His mother's notorious sexual promiscuity had made him doubt his paternity. Casual sex was a common practice for Kings but discouraged in Queens.

His Anne is quite proper. Since their marriage, Charles has cut back to one mistress; he wishes his tiny thin wife would dress more seductively and regally. He points out the mulberry trees planted by his father, Louis XI. The trees, the silk worms, and the silk weavers from Italy, have created a new industry. This is the French way: wear silk, drink wine, enjoy the fruits of the land.

From their coach, the King and Queen see the workers in the fields pause from their work and bow their heads. Louis, besides starting the silk and mining industries, had instituted the Angelus.[9] Ever since Charles could remember, the church bells had rung at noon to call all to a moment's rest and an Ave Maria for peace. Charles and Anne pray for peace and for a child. They should arrive in Tours for supper.

Thursday

Christopher Columbus is on his way to France. Spain has turned her back on the proposal of Cristóbal Colón. Bartolome has not convinced Henry VII of England that his fortunes are across the western seas. Perhaps he is already reasoning with the King of France. Isabella and Fernando are still potential backers; they have provided Christopher with a non-binding retainer of sorts. Their letter instructs all municipalities in Spain to provide him with food and lodging. At least that takes some of the "travail" out of travel.

Journeying from Valencia to Barcelona, looking out across the Mediterranean, he relives his youth in Genoa. Why had his mother named him Cristoforo? For the patron saint of travelers, or because it sits so well on the tongue with Colombo? And Colón, his adopted Spanish name? In Genoa it means colonist or settler. Cristoforo spoke the dialect of Genoa. As an adult, he has mastered Castilian Spanish, and learned to write it. Now he must speak to Charles of France. The young king might finance him. He could become French, Christophe Colombe. Colombe, dove, the dove that brought the branch to Noah in his ark.

God grant him the patience and faith of Noah, and the skill of the dove in finding dry land among the waters. Yes, like his patron saint, Cristoforo will continue to travel and to help travelers. For now, his destination is France and Charles.

Wednesday

Servants are quietly packing and preparing a cushioned litter. Lorenzo de Medici hopes that the quiet at Villa Careggi will restore his health. His legs, painful and swollen with gout, will not support him without assistance. His large bedroom contains an unusual triptych. It is not the usual altar piece of a Madonna with folding wings panels showing saints or patrons. Rather, Lorenzo is surrounded by three large tempera paintings of the *Battle of San Romano*. Uccello had accepted his commission to glorify Florence through this victory. Men and horses and lances are jutting, thrusting, falling and surmounting, giving one the sense of action in space. Lorenzo usually felt energized by these scenes, but now he feels too ill to fight, too weak to stay in Florence, the center of his wool business and banking, his library and sculpture garden. He is ready to leave the Uccello battle scenes in Florence.

Lorenzo is carried two miles into the hills to the villa at Careggi. He asks that a smaller painting accompany him, *Pallas Athena taming Mars*, god of War. Botticelli had been so subtle in his classical references that few realized that this panel was also honoring a victory. Lorenzo was proud that negotiation had brought peace between Naples and Florence. His friendship with King Ferrrante I of Naples had angered Pope Sixtus, but then Sixtus had always looked for a loan he didn't intend to repay, or an excuse to extend his powers. Botticelli's beautiful goddess could personify the beauty of wisdom winning without bloodshed.

"Careggi's country air and quiet will restore you," Lorenzo is told. He hopes for that outcome but remembers that his grandfather died there.

2nd day of the 2nd month, Year of the Rat
124 Ming Dynasty, 4190

The Dragon's birthday heralds the coming of spring. He is an invisible dragon who hibernates all winter and awakens on his birthday. Women in the countryside will not sew or cut all day because they might prick the invisible dragon and that would bring bad luck upon themselves and their village. Instead the women prepare noodles called Dragon's Whiskers to eat and to give as gifts. Their coal fires provide an even heat for cooking.

The men and boys are engaged in rounding up Mongolian ponies. Although the Great Wall has marked the northern security of China for more than 1000 years, recently the Ming emperors have begun encasing the 2,684 miles of mud brick with baked brick and stone. The Great Wall is becoming higher, wider, and more permanent. It is now twenty feet high on the crests of hills, and as high as forty feet on the flat lands. Its sides provide one massive wall for the horse corrals.

Riding and roping in the spring air give the men a huge appetite. Lots of Dragon's Whiskers will be eaten tonight.

1st day of Muharram, 897 A.H.

Islamic New Year

The beginning of a new year is not a major celebration of Islam, but a time to reflect on its beginning and history. Followers of Mohammed have been defeated in Spain, but a few miles south in North Africa, worshippers bow toward Mecca saying:

"God is most Great."

Half way around the world in Malaysia, others continue:

"I testify that Mohammed is the messenger of God."

The powerful Mandingo Empire of central Africa was introduced to Islam more than 160 years ago, and in Timbuktu many still pray five times a day:

"Come to success, in this life and the hereafter."

On the north shore of the Black Sea, the Crimea, some newer converts conclude:

"There is no god except God."

The Islamic calendar dates from 622 A.D., when Mohammed and 70 followers went to Yathhib (now Medinah) to plan a way to reclaim the Kaaba at Mecca from the idol worshippers. Mohammed, a religious man familiar with Jewish and Christian books, built upon their basic beliefs and dictated the lessons God revealed to him through an angel. Not only was he responsible for the Koran but for the Constitution of Medinah, which united the warring clans on the Arabian peninsula.

The first success of this alliance came seven years later when Mohammed and his followers gained access to the

59

Kaaba in Mecca without bloodshed. Islam requires a belief in One God and in Mohammed as his final prophet, but duties include *jihad,* a Holy War against idolaters, but not Jews and Christians.[10] In the next hundred years, Islam spread rapidly to North Africa and into Europe through Spain into southern France. It became established to the east in Persia, and north in Samarkand, Armenia and Syria.

When the Turks were converted to Islam, more territory became Islamic. Four hundred years ago, the Seljuk Turks had squeezed the great Byzantine Empire back to the west side of the straits of the Bosporus. Malik-Shatt had an outstanding vizier, Nizan-al-Mulk, who built a college at Baghdad. Omar Khayyám not only wrote poetry there, but reformed the calendar to twelve lunar months of 29 and 28 days with an extra day added every 11 years to conform to the moon. Poetry, medicine, astronomy, mathematics and architecture flourished under Islam. The Seljuk Turks were eventually defeated by Genghis Khan, but later the Ottoman Turks regained dominance in Anatolia. Just 40 years ago, they succeeded in crossing the Bosporus at Constantinople and defeating the Byzantine Christians.

Fernando and Isabella have completed the long process of removing the Islamic Caliphs from Spain, but the Ottoman Turks have opened a new door in eastern Europe. Around the Indian Ocean, as far as the Malay Peninsula, the Ming emperor of China no longer collects tribute, because the idolaters there have accepted Islam and formed alliances just as Mohammed had taught the Arabs to do 897 Islamic years ago.

Saturday

When Erasmus dips his feather in ink, he writes 1491. For this scholarly churchman and his fellow Augustinian Monks at Steyn, near Gouda, this is the last day of the year. The new year begins on Lady Day, March 25, the Feast of the Annunciation. Many people on the European continent used this system, reasoning that the Christian era started when Jesus began his earthly life in Mary's womb.

Robert Campin and Jan Van Eyck, in their paintings of the *Annunciation*, had even included a tiny Jesus bearing a cross arriving on a beam of light as the angel informs the Virgin of her selection. These minute and precise details were achieved by Flemish painters using oils and oil glazes, and Erasmus found them full of truth. St. Bernard of Clairvaux explained Mary's perpetual virginity with this same illustration; light shining through a window leaves the glass intact and unaltered, just as Mary remained after the Word of God became flesh in her body.

Erasmus is a 24 year old scholar, who reads the commentaries of the saints and the Bible in its original languages, as avidly as he does the ancient philosophers and historians. In fact, he reads whatever he can find or borrow, the bawdy comedies of Aristophanes or the dialogues of Plato. Erasmus has been criticized for his voracious reading interests by the monks who would have him concentrate on the Scriptures. He is writing a spirited defence of his right, or that of any Christian, to read the comedies of the Roman playwright, Terence.

The youthful philosopher pauses from his composition to write to his elder brother Pieter. The brothers share an

61

appetite for books. He writes, "I consider as lovers of books, not those who keep their books hidden in their store chests and never handle them, but those who, by nightly as well as daily use, thumb them, batter them, wear them out, who fill all the margins with annotations of many kinds."

Desiderius Erasmus, must put aside his chosen name, meaning "Beloved of God", when writing to his brother. To Pieter he is still Geerd Geerts, and he would like a letter from home so he ventures, "I believe it would be easier to get blood out of a stone than to coax a letter out of you!"

Saturday

All Jews in Aragon, Castile, and all of Spain must become baptized Christians or leave, never to return. That is the law of the Edict of Exile Isabella and Fernando sign this day. While Moslems will be permitted to stay and worship Allah if they pay taxes, the Jews have no such option. Those not accepting Jesus Christ as Messiah are ordered to leave Spain. They have four months to decide.

April

Sunday

Henry's preparations to invade France are expensive. Today he establishes a custom tax on persons importing tin, copper, wool, hides, honey or tallow.

Thursday

Spring is in the air in Florence. The shadowy interior of Santa Maria Novella offers a respite from the clear, sunny skies. But inside, the fiery reformer Savonarola is continuing the Lenten call for reform. "Christians, do not be seduced by pagan teachings. Aristotle and Plato are rotting in hell. Mothers, keep your daughters dressed modestly. Citizens, do not tolerate the sodomy so publicly practiced in Florence. *Fanciulli* (young men between 5 and 18), do not be misled into these abominable homosexual practices. Be pure! Be chaste!"

The goldsmith returning to his shop on the Ponte Vecchio is moved by the sermon. His apprentice, a handsome youth of 14 is a likely victim of salacious patrons. "I will cut his hair as the priest suggests, and be careful where I send him on deliveries," the craftsman thinks as he returns to his shop on the bridge over the Arno. His grandfather had this same shop. The location is perfect for patrons to be tempted by gold and jewels, but his apprentice should not also be a temptation.

The young man is intently working on an image in wax, his golden curls catching the sunlight as he bends over his work. The master feels some attraction to the boy himself, but quickly says a Pater Noster to put such lustful thought from his mind. He pictures the angelic boy working on a mold for a crucifix with Jesus in agony for our sins; such pieces should sell well with the fervor which Savonarola is inspiring. The apprentice, innocent and proud, shows him a tiny but voluptuous Diana, goddess of the hunt. The master, startled, asks "How do you know the anatomy of women so well?" The boy blushes and lowers his eyes.

That evening a bolt of lightning comes from a cloudless sky and hits the dome of the great cathedral. Chunks of the dome fall through the roof, breaking a marble rib. More than one Florentine feels it is God's judgment. Guilt and responsibility stirred by the reformer become fear and anguish and even repentance.

Friday

Lorenzo the Magnificent, extremely ill with gout, asks for a report on the sudden lightning storm. On learning that the damage to the Cathedral roof was on "his" side of Florence, Lorenzo knows that God is preparing judgment for him.

20th day of the 2nd month, Year of the Rat
155 Ashikaga Dynasty, 4190

In Edo, the cherry trees are bursting with pink blossoms. On this Spring day, these delicate blooms contrast with the brilliance of the saffron robes worn by the Buddhist monks. It is the celebration of the birthday of Buddha.

At Kyoto, children bring armfuls of flowers to mound around the giant reclining Buddha. Today the gilded-bronze statue's smile seems more than just content, but positively happy among the masses of flowers. The usual Japanese household arrangement consists of a single flower with a few leaves carefully arranged and placed in a niche with a small scroll painting of a landscape or animal.

Today to celebrate the birthday of Siddhartha Gautama 2005 years ago in India, flowers are used in profusion. Although the Enlightened One taught that happiness came from renouncing worldly treasures, he rejected self-torture and did not turn against the beauty of nature. His followers in Japan respect Buddha's *dejarma*, or saving truth, finding a middle road where meditation leads to *nirvana*, an acceptance of oneness with all creation.

Sunday

Lorenzo the Magnificent is preparing to meet his creator. Since lightning struck the great dome of the Cathedral in Florence, strange lights have appeared in the sky each evening.

Piero Leoni can not imagine Lorenzo dying at 43 years of age. As his friend and doctor, Leoni prescribes the usual rest and bleeding, and also a special tonic of ground jewels. The Milanese doctor sent by Ludovico Sforza has his powders and remedies, too. Lorenzo seems to know medical efforts are not helping, and Lorenzo calls for Savonarola to come and hear his confession.

This is the first and last meeting of the Catholic reformer and the magnificent prince. When Lorenzo had offered Savonarola the position of Prior of San Marco last year, the monk had accepted, but refused to make the customary call upon his patron, stating that he was accountable only to God. Savonarola's sermons of the past year have attacked the worldly lifestyle that Lorenzo personified.

Lorenzo had married at 19; his bride, Clarice Orsini, was in Rome for their wedding. Lorenzo sent a proxy, stayed in Florence, and staged a lavish tournament in honor of his mistress, Lucretia Donati. The tournament cost 10,000 florins ($360,000). Lorenzo's love for Lucretia lasted all his life, but Clarice was a loyal and fertile partner.

One year after Lorenzo's marriage, his father died, and at 20 he was ruler of Florence. The wealthy banking family

70

of Pazzi rivaled the Medicis and arranged to have Lorenzo and his brother, Giuliano assassinated as they were worshipping on Easter Sunday, 1478. Giuliano died of stab wounds, but Lorenzo fought off his attackers successfully, and thereafter was guarded and cautious. His wife, Clarice, produced 10 children before her death at age 38. She did not live to see the birth of their grandson, Lorenzo, born this very year, 1492.

Lorenzo not only supports Michelangelo, Botticelli, and other artists, reads the classics and writes poetry, but he is also a financial genius. The gold florin with John the Baptist on one side and the red lily, symbol of Florence, on the other, is the accepted standard of exchange in Europe and as far as Tunis and Istanbul. His letters of exchange bear the motto, "Christ help you". Issued from the 33 banks in Florence, this "paper money" is as good as gold in London, Naples, Cologne, Geneva, Bruges, Antwerp, Rome, Venice, Avignon or Sevilla.

A few years ago, Lorenzo negotiated a treaty with Henry VII of England to import wool. In Florence, the 270 woolen workshops outnumbered those for wood (84), silk (83), and jewelry (44). The special Florentine red dye for wools and silks is reserved for Cardinals of the Church. Lorenzo is exceedingly proud that his 16 year old son is a Cardinal. Pope Innocent VIII had given the red hat to the young Giovanni when he was 13.

Is it any wonder that Lorenzo refers to Savonarola as "the one honest priest" when he asks that he be brought to his bedside? Girolamo Savonarola is the son and grandson of physicians, and had studied medicine for a time. To this uncompromising reformer, who only fears the God of Eternity, Lorenzo makes his confession and receives the last rites of the Roman Catholic Church.

71

Though Savonarola had predicted last year, "I must remain and he must depart", he does not seek a worldly victory. He asks Lorenzo if he loves and fears God and is sorry for his sins. The friar asks the prince if he is ready to meet Jesus face to face, if God chooses to take him now. Lorenzo asks Savonarola to pray with him. While onlookers cry, the Magnificent Prince of the Renaissance is gently guided to eternity with the Prince of Peace by one who answers only to God, and God has put compassion in his heart at this hour.

Lorenzo dies to this earth. His death fits perfectly with Savonarola's Lenten theme. "The Sword of the Lord is hanging over Florence." Lorenzo goes to his judgment. What of the city? What of the Medici family?

Tuesday

Lorenzo de Medici's body is taken from his hillside villa down the winding roads to the church of San Marco in Florence. After the lightning and the strange lights, the people seem almost prepared for this sad procession. But some gossip about his doctors. Where is Piero Leoni, and where is the Milanese doctor? A dead man has no need of a physician, but neither is anywhere to be seen. Could the Sforza ruler have sent an assassin in the guise of a doctor? Sforza is Force, and Ludovico is hungry for power.

The maid goes to the well for water and calls for help. Another death befalls Careggi. Piero Leoni's body is pulled from the well. As a friend, has he committed suicide in despair at Lorenzo's death? Or as a doctor, has he been murdered by his rival from Milan to keep him from telling an awful truth?

Wednesday

After a Requiem Mass, Lorenzo's body is laid to rest in the Medici tomb next to his brother, Giuliano. The Council of Seventy meets and waives the age restriction so that twenty year old Piero can replace his father. He is a pale imitation of his father, although his handsome appearance makes many hope for greatness. Piero is married to Alfonsina Orsini, but his sexual and temporal excesses are not just decried by Savonarola, but shock local libertines. Since Piero de Medici is not very intelligent and is influenced by flattery, his leadership potential is small.

Thursday

Savonarola announces that God has judged Florence, and its people must expect their punishment.

Palm Sunday

Christopher Columbus is back in Spain. He was on his way to seek the support of Charles of France and his bride, Anne of Brittany. But Isabella and Fernando have sent couriers to request his presence. Bartolome Columbus, has arrived in France, expecting to meet his brother. He has been in England more than three years trying to persuade Henry VII to finance this Enterprise of the Indies. Maybe Charles will be the royal patron.

Tuesday

Fernando is signing papers at the Alhambra. The nearby city of Santa Fe has finally succumbed to his siege. And, oh yes, let us sign papers for Cristóbal Colón. Let him find men and ships in Palos and sail west to find Cipangu. Since Luis de Santangel, keeper of the king's purse, is willing to put his own money on such an important undertaking, and Isabella has even offered her jewels as security, Fernando can do no less than give his financial support. So begins 3 1/2 weeks of planning in Granada.

Easter Sunday

Jonathan Whitanner lifts his voice in praise. His baritone part is written on an erasable waxed board. The sopranos, altos, tenors and basses all have different tunes and timing, but the words repeat, words of praise to God. Their choir director, Thomas Ashwell, has written music as mighty as the words, a real triumph in polyphonic music. Without being a distraction to worshippers, Ashwell must signal the singers when to begin, for each music board only shows one part and not the others. The Salisbury Cathedral Choir is presenting this premier performance before the Easter Sunday High Mass begins.

High in the 404 foot spire of the Cathedral, the bells chime nine. In the old days, the hour was terse, the time for mid-morning prayers; on Sunday, the hour for High Mass. People have been coming into the Cathedral for more than an hour and continue to arrive. For many, the bells in the steeple and the sun are their only time keepers.

Now the choir relaxes with familiar music. This polyphonic mass is not an Ashwell composition, but one written by Gilbert Bannister. When Bannister died five years ago, the Bishop realized that his great gift for church music might die with him, and provided for his choral music to be recorded in a large vellum book.

Visitors from London have commented on the beauty of the Sarum Liturgy; Thomas Ashwell has continued to keep Salisbury preeminent in Tudor music.

Monday

For their wedding, JONATHAN WHITANNER and MARGARET of Sarum ride together in a two-wheeled coach pulled by JONATHAN's horse. MARGARET's father, a coachmaker, made it as a wedding present, comfortable but not luxurious. Just recently, English coachmakers have started to make the new four-wheeled carriages. MARGARET's father made one for the Earl of Salisbury, and it caused lots of comment.

Salisbury Cathedral, where they will be married, is unique among the fine Gothic cathedrals of Europe. No city shops and houses crowd around it; it is surrounded by an open green plain. Not just its steeple, but the entire church, from its lead roof to the saints carved in stone on its walls, can be seen from the rolling hills that surround it.

MARGARET comments, "From my home in Sarum, the Cathedral seems so small to me, almost like a toy. But as we draw near, it is so tall and majestic. The circle stones at Stonehenge are as tall as three men, but this must be as tall as 100 men!"

"I feel as proud as 100 men to have you be my wife," JONATHAN replies. MARGARET's remarks seem to have put the church above Druid practices, which is a comfort to the serious, conventional groom. Certainly the church has greatly influenced their wedding day.

JONATHAN and MARGARET were betrothed seven weeks ago with an agreement notarized at church covering his property and her dowry and its disposition should one of them die or the marriage fail. The church required their bans be announced for three weeks, but does not permit marriages during Lent except in special circumstances. The church also requires brides to be twelve and grooms, fourteen, not related, and both consenting. Back in the days of Henry III, men used to kidnap their wives, so the church acted to stop this barbaric practice. MARGARET is a mature sixteen. This morning, her mother dressed her in a linen chemise, a silk dress with a velvet surcoat, and a new cape. Her father has provided a dowry of linens, a feather bed, and the fine coach they are riding in. He wonders if he has been too generous, for MARGARET's younger sisters will need dowries, too.

Their families and friends meet the couple at the door to the Cathedral. MARGARET carries some spring flowers and the traditional wheat stocks. She wears a small veil fastened with a gold clip. At a side altar, they exchange vows. JONATHAN puts the gold wedding band on each of her four fingers saying, "In the name of the Father, the Son, the Holy Spirit," with a finger for each, and ending with her third finger left hand, "I thee wed."

While the couple signs the wedding register, the guests hurry to their new home. The WHITANNER family has been in the leather business in Salisbury for several generations. JONATHAN's grandfather has moved into his son's house, and has given his house to JONATHAN. MARGARET's parents call Salisbury, New Sarum. People had lived at Old Sarum, two miles up the hill, long before the time of King Arthur, but Salisbury had its beginning as an important town when the Cathedral was built 150 years ago. JONATHAN's house is well situated for his business in fine leathers.

The guests have brought gifts and food, especially currant cakes and biscuits. As JONATHAN and MARGARET approach the threshold of their home, their friends break large flat wheat biscuits over the bride's head. The groom tries to protect her, but MARGARET is a spirited woman.

When her youngest sister throws a currant cake at her, MARGARET dodges deftly. It's all in good fun.

Russian Orthodox Easter

Russian Orthodox Easter is a good time to visit the Kremlin in Moscow. Ivan the Great has ruled 30 years since he was 22 years old. He has hired Italian architects to replace the old wooden buildings of the Kremlin with a stone palace and two new churches. To protect his imperial capital, Ivan authorized 1 1/2 miles of stone walls to enclose the Kremlin.

Ivan has proclaimed himself Tsar, a successor to the Byzantine emperors, the founder of a third Rome. First, to the East, he had defeated the Mongols, descendants of Genghis Khan. For more than 250 years, this Golden Horde had ruled Russia. Ten years ago, Ivan moved West, laid siege to Novgorod, and it fell. This provided Ivan access to Central and Western Europe through the Gulf of Finland. His realm stretches from the Arctic to the Ural mountains in the South. His success is due to military maneuvers, diplomacy and trickery. Ivan's eldest son is married to a Moldavian princess, and his daughter, Yelena, is married to Alexander, son of Casimir IV, King of Poland and Lithuania. At 52, Ivan has come a long way since he was Grand Prince Ivan III of Moscow. His early conquests over the Mongols and Tatars brought political prestige to Moscow, which had long been a stronghold of the Russian Orthodox Church. Ivan's first wife died when he was 27; five years later in 1472, he married Sophia Paloelogus, niece of the last Byzantine Emperor of Constantinople, and ward of the Pope. Sophia is intelligent, witty, and ambitious. At their marriage, she signed herself 'Imperial Princess of Byzantium', while her husband, the Grand

Prince of Moscow was in reality a vassal of the Khan of the Golden Horde. After defeating them decisively in 1480, Ivan added the title "Autocrat", and Moscow became Russia.

Sophia's influence appears in the addition of the double-headed eagle of Byzantium to the state crest and seal. Ivan became the Tsar and she the Tsarina. Venetian craftsmen directed by Alberto Fioraventi and Pietro Antonio are rebuilding the Kremlin with a new palace and cathedral. Ivan's taxes on fur traders and spoils of war help to finance these projects.

The Russian Orthodox Church, like all Eastern Orthodox churches, had broken with Rome over John's gospel, chapter 15, verse 26. The Orthodox belief is that the Holy Spirit proceeds from the Father, as this verse states, and that Rome had added "and from the Son" to their creed. However that belief affected conscience, many other organizational differences made the separation more permanent. Each Orthodox church is tied to a country and independent of the others. Priests may marry before they are ordained, but bishops and monks must be unmarried. Laymen share in worship as readers and deacons. The monasteries of Russia have huge holdings of land but also feed the poor and provide education in arts and letters.

When Sophia was escorted to Moscow for her marriage to Ivan, her protector, Pope Sixtus IV hoped to unite the Roman and Russian Orthodox Catholics. Moscow had long been a stronghold of the Orthodox Church, and the Bishop had no trouble in gathering forces to prevent the Latin crosses from entering his dominion. Sophia was welcome, but her Papist escorts were turned away at the gates.

Orthodox Easter is a time for gift giving and celebration. The resurrection of Jesus Christ is given more emphasis than his earthly birth. The Russian Orthodox Church prohibits sexual relations during the six weeks of Lent, and also imposes dietary abstinence and fasting. A way to appreciate God's gifts is to forego them for a time. For Easter in Moscow, trees are leafing, snow is melting, flowers are beginning to bloom. Nature reflects a message of life rising from the dead.

The Uspenskii Cathedral is one of two new churches in the Kremlin and is dedicated to the Assumption of the Virgin Mary. So, she is pictured in the large icon just to the left of the center doors of the iconostasis. Many icons, or pictures of Jesus and the saints, form the iconostasis, an elaborate wall separating the main cathedral from the holy apse where only priests are permitted. These holy men with full beards, domed hats, and long robes, leave their holy of holies through the central doors and enter the sanctuary. Assistants carry Russian crosses, incense, candles, and portable icons. The Bishop's domed hat and collar are of gold, and he is seated on a throne to the right of the altar. Ivan and Sophia, the Tsar and Tsarina, are worshipping at Uspenskii Cathedral today rather than the royal chapel. Here, and in every home, the icons of the saints appear ethereal and spiritual by the flickering candle light. The saints give hope for a life after death and for their help in intercession in the affairs of this world.

May

Tuesday

English roads are muddy when it rains, dusty when it's dry, and full of hazards. Their maintenance is at the whim of the large land owners, nobility and monasteries. On the well traveled routes, post-houses are a recent addition. King Henry sends official government mail by this system. Privacy and security are the main considerations, but also promptness and efficiency. Sealed documents and some private correspondence are routed through the post-houses. The regular riders even bring reports on road conditions. Hermits living in remote areas extract tolls for bridges they maintain or fees for giving directions or pulling a cart from the mud.

The roads to Canterbury Cathedral are old and well traveled by pilgrims. St. Augustine, Apostle to the English in 597 and first Archbishop of Canterbury, established this site; his chair is still revered. But for the past 321 years, the tomb of Saint Thomas has been the primary goal. Thomas á Becket, Archbishop of Canterbury, was murdered here in 1170, and the first penitent to come to his tomb was a sorrowful, barefoot King Henry II whose men had killed Becket. Around his tomb in Trinity Chapel are stained glass windows depicting the miracles attributed to the martyred saint.[12] Buried nearby are Edward, the Black Prince and Henry IV. The practical pilgrim, having made the journey, prays to all three to intercede and grant a miracle.

Tuesday

The road is never too long or too rough when a holy place beckons. Moslems go to Mecca. Hindus and Buddhists go to the navel of the world, Mount Kailas. Christian pilgrimages focus on Jerusalem, Rome, and Santiago de Compostella. Jerusalem is unavailable this year; the Moslems there (Mamelukes) will tolerate the Jews coming from Spain, but are prepared to fight Crusaders. Travel planners do not recommend Rome; the crime in the streets has been increasing the past seven years.

"The road is never too rough or too long when you go to Santiago de Compostella," the Parisian tour guide tells the pilgrims assembled at the Tower of St. Jacques. The music, the blessings of priest, and the cavalry escort lends a holiday excitement as thousands of people, from nobles and knights to common folk and criminals, are organized into travel groups. All wear identical heavy capes, which also serve as their bedrolls, and a hat decorated with the cockle shells emblematic of Saint James. Each carries a tall staff with a water gourd attached.

The Tower of St. Jacques is small and unimpressive compared to the Cathedral of Notre Dame just across the Seine. From the bridge that links them, it is just a four minute walk to either place. The massive cathedral with its flying buttresses, twelfth-century stained glass, and Gothic sculpture is a well known landmark of Paris, but the Tower of St. Jacques sits on a small hill, and is easily found by the pilgrims who gather here. The nearby church of St. Merri is convenient for last minute prayers. The faithful light candles and visit all the chapels in the

87

ambulatory, kneeling a moment at each to petition another saint for traveling mercies. The pickpockets find the flickering candlelight and crowded church a better place to ply their trade than the sunlit square around the tower.

The many groups leaving today plan to make the 900 mile journey to Compostella, Spain, in time to celebrate St. James Day, July 25. On that day in 812, a hermit saw strange lights in the sky that led him to a field. He dug there and found the perfectly preserved body of St. James, the Apostle who had brought Christianity to Spain right after his cousin, Jesus of Nazareth, rose from the dead. Diego, as James is known in Spain, became its patron saint, and began to appear miraculously on a white horse in battles helping the Spanish army defeat the Moslems. San Diego effectively countered the most effective relic of the Moslems, the arm of Mohammed, which they kept at the Mosque of Cordoba when it wasn't being carried into battle. San Diego became abbreviated to Santiago, and his still uncorrupted body resting under the altar at the Romanesque church at Compostella continues to work miracles for the faithful.

Latin for James is *Jacobus*, and French is *Jacques*. This international pilgrimage has been popular for hundreds of years. A travel guide written in 1130 describes the abbeys, churches, and shrines along the route for the hundreds of thousands of people who attempt it each year.[13] The 300 year old Order of Santiago de Compostella, good Christian men free of any Jewish or Moslem ancestry and pledged to be faithful to their wives, maintains order as this throng moves south.

Other pilgrims will start from Vezelay and Arles, but by the time the Paris travelers cross the Pyrénées mountains into Roncesvalles, the additions will simply replace those who have died and were buried along the way. Further

88

along, some Spaniards join the group in Pamplona, and others do a thriving business in selling certificates that prove one has completed the pilgrimage. These are especially popular with the criminals who have chosen the trip to Santiago de Compostella as a kind of probation in lieu of jail and can return to the judge with a proof of completion without further hardship.

The happy band starting in Paris by the Tower of St. Jacques is not thinking of the sandals that will wear out, the thieves along the road, or the polluted water that will kill so many. They offer these trials to God, so when they arrive in the presence of James the Apostle, they will be worthy to ask his help and worship under the giant silver censer that swings across the ceiling of the Cathedral of Santiago de Compostella spreading incense over the road-weary pilgrims.[14]

Tuesday

"The snow mountain is the navel of the world where snow leopards dance," so Mila, the Cotton Clad[15] wrote in his *Hundred Thousand Songs of Mount Kailas.* Pilgrims come on an individual quest to this axis of the world, the center of all creation, the mountain home of Lord Kailas and his wife Parvati. Four rivers start here and invite seekers of peace and seekers of power to follow them to their source, climbing higher and higher to sacred Mount Kailas. This pilgrimage to the Himalaya mountains may take months, like Santiago de Compostella, or even years.

The pilgrims dress in felt coats lined with sheepskin wool, and sheepskin hats and carry prayer beads. Their attire contrasts to the guru and poet Mila the Cotton Clad, who had such psychic heat that he was impervious to the cold. He is admired because he was able to renounce the limitations of the physical world and experience nirvana in one lifetime. The worshippers chant, "Om mani padme hum," or simply "Om" or "Ma".

After coming so far, most do not climb the 22,028-foot Mount Kailas, but circle it at elevations of 15,000 and 18,000 feet. They draw strength from seeing its striking, snow-capped, triangular top. From four shrines, they view the mountain, pray and meditate, and experience an awakening. At one stop, the women anoint an ancient Dolma stone with butter. Some plunge into the icy waters of Lake Manasa. To experience Mount Kailas transports the accomplished yogi and inspires all to a sacred awareness. Reincarnation continues until the individual at last loses himself to the universe.

90

Tuesday

Another mountain pilgrimage site is among mysterious natural monoliths in Catalonia. Like Kailas, the mountain itself, although only 4,000 feet high, looks like a special sculpture from the hand of God. Like Compostella, a miracle occurred here which helped inspire the Spanish to defeat the Moslems.

In 880, a hermit found a wooden statue of the Virgin Mary and Jesus, carved by Saint Luke and blackened by time, in a cave where it was hidden when Islam swept north through Spain. The 2 1/2 foot statue inspired Benedictine monks to build a monastery among these rocky peaks. The black virgin was credited with many miracles, and pilgrims continued to come from near and far. Montserrat became the religious and cultural center for Catalonians, who are keeping their language in spite of Isabella promoting Castilian.

The Benedictine monks at Montserrat lead a disciplined life, worshipping six times a day, singing in Gregorian chant. Crusaders brought them the Holy Grail, the cup that Jesus used at the Last Supper. The monks stay on their holy mountain, tend to their precious relics, and the European world comes to them.

Montserrat is a few days journey from Barcelona, and Canterbury is a few days from London. Like the Canterbury travelers whom Geoffrey Chaucer immortalized in 1388, pilgrims to Montserrat find these spring outings a time to share stories as well as seek blessings.

91

Inca weaving, in private collection.

Bridges and roads are a specialty of the Incas. In 1492, from their capital at Cuzco, they send goods and messages along the Andes mountains and western coasts from north of the equator to close to the tip of South America. None of these mountain and coastal people have developed a written language, but the art of ceramics had flourished with the Moche. The Paracas, 1000 years before the Incas, had brought weaving to an excellence that is still admired. The Incas had united and absorbed these ethnic groups and their arts in the last 50 years and relied on their roads to keep their control and authority. Inca roads depend at least as much on the ability of their society to concentrate labor as on the technology of the actual construction.

Everyone works. Farmers, spinners, weavers, builders and warriors are the main occupations. Warriors wear masks and little else into battle. The masks indicate spiritual connections. Human sacrifice is common, even in peace time. The Inca receives cooperation and awe. He is the Sun God's representative on earth.

Farmers grow potatoes, cotton, maize, squash, and chile peppers. Near the coasts, pineapples, peanuts, and avocados grow. Farmers make lots of chicha, the native beer for relaxing when work was done. Tobacco and coca leaves provide a further escape.

When building a house, a llama fetus is buried at the corner for good luck. The public works are outstanding. The construction with monolithic stones of walled cities, terraced farms, and public buildings requires coordinated effort, as does the maintenance of roads and bridges. In this land of many earthquakes, the permanence is enhanced by the trapezoid door openings. The narrower top offers more stability.

This day, the Inca ruler, Huayna Cápac, will go to see for himself if there is damage from the shaking that has awakened everyone early this morning. Runners have already brought some reports of damage north of Cuzco. Carried from the palace in a litter of gold, the Inca is a dazzling sight in the clear mountain air. Messages continue to arrive, but even with the relay runners stationed about two miles apart, it takes a few days for news to arrive. The Inca rules a territory four times as large as the Italian peninsula, where the Duke of Milan, Doge of Venice, the Medici of Florence, the Pope in Rome, and the Prince of Naples, are jockeying for power over each other and Sienna, Genoa, or Palermo.

The golden litter is carried past the golden temple of the sun and the vast complex where the virgins of the Inca live and tend to their weaving. Once clear of the center of Cuzco, the litter carriers break into a trot. In a land without the wheel or the horse, distance running is cultivated. Soon they come to a landslide that has destroyed a corn field. The road has already been repaired. Now winding down a narrow path carved into the side of a mountain, some stray rocks and a few boulders give evidence of the quake. Horses, had they lived in the New World, would have done well on this road, but wheels would be useless on this steep descent.

Huayna Cápac looks ahead to the bridge; it appears to be unaffected. Fiber suspension bridges are the perfect short cut over a steep chasm. Built of twisted fibers braided into huge cables, these bridges are an outstanding engineering and public works project. Children, excited by the swaying and the long drop below, are closely supervised. Repairs and renovations are frequent. But in a land of earthquakes, the flexibility of the design is an asset. Nearing the bridge, the Inca halts his carriers and emerges from the golden litter in a tunic with hawk motifs in black and yellow on a red ground. The gold collar he wears catches the sunlight with such brilliance that even the circling hawks and condors take a glance in his direction, then resume their hunting.

Birds and emperor together are drawn to the sight of two swift runners approaching the bridge from the west. They carry fresh fish and mussels from the Pacific Ocean. Their pace doesn't slow as they gracefully trot across the suspension bridge. The Inca stops these two, and is assured that damage is even less at the sea side. Messengers carry a *quipu*, a cord with many smaller strings and knots, to serve as a memory guide. Incas and the former tribes have the concept of zero, and knotted strings have obvious uses for numerical information, but the *quipu* also serves to preserve oral histories and current news.

Satisfied with his outing and proud of this bridge, the Inca reenters his golden box to be carried back to his palace. The fish will arrive first and be cooked to his liking.

The golden litter of Huayna Cápac returns to Cuzco. As dazzling as the Inca ruler appears in his travels, he is a minor example of the treasure at the Coricancha, the temple of the sun at Cuzco. Gold and the Sun God, Inti, are intermingled. The Incas conquered the Chimor kingdom 45 years ago, and, admiring their goldsmiths' work, have enslaved them to serve their Sun God. The conquered Chimu craftsmen sometimes alloy the pure gold with copper or silver. They employ the lost wax process to produce fine details. Thousands of gold plaques are linked together to make a poncho. Golden collars, tweezers, combs, or gloves might be for this life or for the hereafter. For the Inca, like their predecessors, the Moche and the Chimus, have elaborate burials to prepare for a life after death.

95

Priests of Inti pray that the gold seeds in the mountains will grow, and their prayers seem to be answered. Each year 200 tons of gold arrived in Cuzco, the political and religious capital. A herd of life-sized llamas, each made of 350 pounds of gold, are accompanied by their golden kids and shepherds, life-size men of gold. Yet size is not all; delicate spiders, tiny mice and lizards also live in this fantasy world. Even the dirt and stones are fashioned of silver and gold in the Garden of the Sun. The treasure is for Inti, the Sun God, but it is also personally linked to Huayna Cápac, the Inca ruler. His son Atahualpa is beginning his own gold collection in anticipation of his future role. When Huayna Cápac dies, Atahualpa plans to rule and to build a golden tribute to his power and the power of the Sun God. However, his brother, Huascar, is not so enmeshed in this religious practice. His interests are the building of fortresses and roads. Huascar travels the vast network of roads and identifies with the people who live 1,000 miles from Cuzco. When Huayna Cápac dies, there will be civil war.

Saturday

Cristóbal, Fernando, and Isabella, what a trio! All in their 40's, all attempting to grasp and enjoy a mature victory.

Fernando has married the heiress of Castile and schemed and fought to conquer the Moors. His style is admired by Machiavelli, a young Florentine who is collecting examples for his book *The Prince*, which extols using deceit and force to govern and control. Fernando enjoys his power, his political and his sexual conquests. His legitimate heirs can also further his political goals. His youngest daughter, Catalina of Aragon might be a good match for Henry VII's son, Arthur.

Isabella's goals are not earthly but eternal. She is chaste and thanks God for the children He has granted her after many miscarriages. God has also granted them victory over Islam; the Caliphs of Sevilla and Granada are gone. Soon the Jews must leave or convert. Isabella prays for all to be Christians, and Fernando sees opportunities to gain more temporal power. Thanks to Isabella of Castile, the first grammar printed in any language is a reality this year. Antonio de Nebrija has written it, it has been published in Zaragosa, and the language is Castilian. Fernando can conquer, but language can unify the Spanish.

Today they sign final papers for Cristóbal Colón. His goals are as idealistic as Isabella's and as worldly as Fernando's. The contract these three sign today grants Colón the title "Admiral of the Ocean" and "Governor General" of all lands and islands discovered by him. These titles are hereditary; Cristóbal has a son being educated by

97

the monks at Palos. Also, the contract provides that he will retain 10% of all treasure reaching Spain from his journeys. He is a dreamer who has fought for ships and provisions, but also for a future of fame and fortune.

Fernando wonders if he has bargained for 90% of nothing. Isabella has a pure faith that God will provide. The Admiral of the Ocean bids goodbye to Granada to go to Palos for ships and men.

Wednesday

May is a fine month for travel, snows have melted, summer heat is yet to come. In 1492, pilgrims brave poor roads and unknown dangers, journeymen-artisans move on to new challenges. Travel by water is easier than by land, except in the Americas, where without the wheel or the horse, roads and bridges are dependable. No obstacle will deter Columbus from going overland to Palos to outfit his ships and see his son Diego.

Monday

Look at the face of Albrecht Dürer. The greatest artist in German history is 21 years old today. His youthful indecisiveness shows in the self-portrait he has just completed in pen and ink. This is not the first or last time he records his image. From a child in a cap, to an elegant beardless youth, to a Christ-like bearded face surmounting a body dressed in un-Christ-like opulence, he records his growing self-confidence. The humanist spirit of the Renaissance of the north is exemplified by this emphasis on the self-portrait, which Dürer pioneered.

Albrecht also did portraits of his parents. He is named for his father, a goldsmith of Nuremberg. He is the third of 18 children born to his pious and hard-working parents. His home in Nuremberg is small but among the most comfortable in Europe, with a tiled kitchen and shuttered windows. His mother, Barbara, wishes the little house were more crowded. She has buried 15 children. Albrecht's little two year old brother, Hans, is the third child to be given that name by his parents. Barbara prays that he will be as healthy and strong as his 21 year old brother.

Albrecht Dürer, the journeyman artist, is tall, broad-shouldered, and strong. His hands are elegant with long tapering fingers. His eyes are penetrating. Details of owls, rabbits, squirrels flow from those eyes to his hand. A broad landscape, accented by trees, and the details of a violet appear in his sketches. He can work and learn in Basel. Though he will return to Nuremberg, Albrecht Dürer is gaining confidence to travel wherever his art leads him.

Monday

Cristóbal Colón dismounts his horse and walks into the courtyard of the Franciscan monastery of La Rabida. A monk recognizes him at once.

"Señor Colón, welcome. I will tell Brother Antonio you are here."

"Thank you, and please tell my son, Diego, too," he replies.

It's been a long trip by land, but now Cristóbal can finally get ships for the trip he has been planning for ten years. The spring flowers in the courtyard are lovely, but no sight is as welcome as twelve-year-old Diego. The boy comes running, and Colón stands and opens his arms to enfold his son.

They talk of Diego's school, this monastery where he has lived since he was five, after his mother had died.

"Father, will you be able to stay?"

"Yes," interrupted Brother Antonio de Marchend who joins them, "will you be staying with us? You are most welcome, my son."

"I will be pleased to stay here while I prepare my ships to sail west," Colón replies. "Yes, the King and Queen have given royal orders for ships, men and provisions."

Diego brightens, "May I go with you?"

The priest puts his hand on the boy's shoulder, "Patience, young man. Let your father speak."

"Diego, King Fernando has invited you to come to court and be a page to Prince Juan. It will be good for you to learn the ways of rulers, for when I return I shall

101

be Admiral of the Ocean and Governor General of all lands I find. These titles will be yours after I die, and for your sons, also." Cristóbal continues, "Antonio, you know Palos. I need to present my orders to the proper authorities."

"I will help you," the padre replies, "but first you must rest, and then tell me how you finally convinced the King and the Queen." Brother Antonio is an astronomer who has taken great interest in Colón's maps and charts, as well as being a teacher of Diego.

"We will sleep here tonight, but Diego and I must make another visit this afternoon. May he be excused from his remaining classes today?"

Permission granted, the father and son share a horse to visit Cristóbal's natural son Fernando, who is 3 1/2 and living with his mother Beatriz Enriquez. She provides the only sense of home that the adventurous Cristóbal has. He promises he will give her cousin a good job in his exploration. Diego says that he would rather stay there than be a court page while his father is gone, and Beatriz agrees.

Wednesday

Diego Rodriguez Prieto, Alcalde Mayor of Palos, and Cristóbal Colón have called a meeting at the church of San Jorge. Colón reads his orders to the authorities and citizens assembled. The King and Queen decree that Palos provide them with two caravels armed at their expense to be put at the disposal of Cristóbal Colón to go to "certain parts of the Ocean Sea on some errands required by our service." The city has ten days to comply.

Among the citizens are the Pinzón brothers, sailors of some reputation. Martin Pinzón and his son went to Rome two years ago where they consulted with the Papal astronomer. Pinzón was encouraged by Innocent VIII to sail west to Cathay, but not financially supported. Martin speaks to the newcomer and the crowd, "May I ask which 'certain parts of the Ocean Sea' you are planning to sail?"

Colón produces Paolo Toscanelli's map and his own charts and makes his presentation. Some citizens scoff, but Pinzón believes in sailing west to Cathay. He is just irritated that this upstart outsider has royal backing and has pre-empted him. Cristóbal concludes by quoting the *Imago Mundi* by Cardinal Pierre d'Ailly, "The sea between the end of Spain on the west and the beginning of the Indies on the east is navigated in a very few days if the wind is favorable."

103

10th day of Rabi I, 897 A.H.

Qaitbay, the Sultan of Cairo, rules a nation where slavery is a pre-requisite to power.[16] The Mamelukes are Islamic Turks who were enslaved by Genghis Khan as he swept south past the Black Sea more than 250 years ago. Khan sold them to the Caliph of Cairo, where they were valued as a fierce army which defeated the Christian Crusaders, and as bodyguards to royalty.

The Mamelukes came to power in 1250 when the Sultan's wife concealed his death and ruled for several months while her son was summoned. The son was disliked and murdered, and Shajar-al-durr, his mother, continued to rule, but this time she was elected by her army of Mamelukes. The Sultan of Baghdad objected to a woman ruling; she had been a gift from his harem. So she married her commander-in-chief and eventually abdicated in his favor.

For the past 24 years, Qaitbay has ruled the Mameluke Empire, which encompasses the Nile River valley, and the lands east to Mecca, and north to Palestine, Syria and Cypress. Qaitbay himself was a slave, purchased by Barsbay, the sultan who conquered Cypress. Ironically, the soldier/slave Mamelukes, and Qaitbay in particular, have sponsored all forms of artistic activities.

Metal workers make swords and helmets, but also candlesticks, trays, bowls, and boxes to store the Koran. They excel in bronze inlaid with silver and gold, and use the elegant Arabic letters and floral motifs to convey messages in what appears to western eyes as geometric designs.

Like the Egyptian Pharaohs of old, Qaitbay began building himself a tomb soon after he came to power. It is a showcase of Mameluke art, decorated with colorful tiles and inlaid stones, furnished with carpets in which stylized palms, papyrus and cypresses repeat in vivid colors, and completed by the fabulous Mameluke glass. Stained glass windows and the graceful oil burning lamps, suspended by metal chains, are etched and enameled in blues, reds, and yellows and highlighted with gold leaf. Like all Islamic art, living beings are not represented, and the calligraphy often gives glory to Allah.

The mausoleum sits completed and waiting, and now the Sultan thinks more of death. The plague has recently killed his wife and daughter, and continues to spread from the crowded streets of Cairo throughout his Sultanate, killing thousands. His son, Muhammed, lives, but an aging Qaitbay wonders if he will be able to hold the throne he inherits.[17] A slave can become Sultan, rising through the ranks of the Mameluke army. By proving his competence, the slave is more likely to have popular support than one who inherits his position. Slavery in Mameluke Egypt is not subjugation, but an invitation to the "owned" individual to prove his worth.

Qaitbay's troubles began when he took sides in the fight between Djem and Bayazid, brothers who each wanted to rule the Ottoman Turks after the death of their father, Mohammed II. Qaitbay supported Djem, and the victorious Bayazid attacked his northern borders and captured Tarsus. Mameluke soldiers stopped the Turks, but Qaitbay relinquished territory and opted for peace. Now this plague has killed and continues to kill great numbers of people. Qaitbay, the great reviver of Mameluke arts is facing a new challenge. Perhaps if he sends more candlesticks and lamps to the mosque at Medina, Allah will again bless this former slave and his people.

June

Tuesday

The body of Casimir IV, King of Poland and Lithuania is resting in a coffin at the door of the Cathedral of Our Lady at Krakow. The magnificent Gothic cathedral is filled with his subjects, family, friends and enemies. For more than fifty years, he ruled first Lithuania and then Poland. The first half of his rule was marked by many successes and peace. He established a Diet for nobles to participate in, and firmly controlled warring families. Recently, threats from within and without have made it impossible to extend his territory through his sons.

The Roman Catholic Bishop appears at the front of the church and the congregation stands. In the front rows are Casimir's widow, Elizabeth of Austria, surrounded by eleven of their thirteen children and their families. The eldest, Ladislas Jagello has been King of Bohemia for twenty years. Two years ago, he overextended his power into Hungary and now is vulnerable. The Bishop is Casimir and Elizabeth's fifth son, Fredick. A tall, handsome man, he strides down the long aisle to the waiting casket accompanied by altar boys with candles and incense.

His brother, John Albert is already favored by the Poles to be their King, and brother Alexander is preferred by the Lithuanians. The Radziwills and other ambitious families see their chance to expand their personal fortunes in the coming months and years. The litany to bury the King is a formality for them, the power they seek is real.

More citizens are seated and kneeling at the back of the Cathedral. Nicolaus Copernicus and other students from the University of Krakow have come out of curiosity and to pay their respects to the King. Twenty-year-old Nicolaus has been a student in Krakow for a year and a half; mathematics is his field. The Bishop notices Veit Stoss, the great sculptor of the altar and choir stalls of this Cathedral. The Bishop has already commissioned him to do a tomb for his father.

Arriving at the casket, Fredick sprinkles holy water over his father and prays, "Eternal rest grant him, O Lord, and let perpetual light shine upon him."

Tears well in this Bishop's eyes as he turns to lead the procession with the coffin to the altar. How will God judge a father who contributed to his own son's death? The youngest brother, named Casimir like his father, had refused to lead an army against Hungary, and the King had him imprisoned. He lived ten years in wretched conditions and died when he was twenty-five. People were beginning to call him a saint.

The casket rests at the front of the church and the litany continues. The choir stalls are empty; black drapes have partially covered the carving. Veit Stoss's artistry is seen in the forty foot altar depicting scenes from the life of Mary. The Bishop lifts his hands and prays for forgiveness "Through the intercession of the Blessed Mary, ever a Virgin, and all the saints." The Mother of God, like the perfect Lady of the medieval knight, has inspired devotion and cathedrals throughout Christendom.

At the conclusion of the Mass, the coffin is opened. The family stays seated as those behind them file past for one last look at their King. They exit through a side chapel and out the south door.

Veit Stoss and his oldest child, fourteen-year-old Guntrum, linger on the porch. The students from Krakow University notice him.

"Look, Nicolaus, that must be Veit Stoss," WERNER KOSCIOSKO indicates the middle-aged man.

"Should I know him?" Nicolaus asks.

"He is the sculptor who did the altar and choir stalls for our cathedral," WERNER chides.

As more students file out, Nicolaus Copernicus makes way for them and draws closer to Stoss.

"Sir, may I be so bold as to tell you that your carving is magnificent," Nicolaus begins. Since there is no response, he continues, "You are Veit Stoss, aren't you?"

"Indeed I am," Stoss replies, "but I feel speechless at your sudden praise. Are you a student of the arts?"

"No, no. This is my friend WERNER who reads philosophy, and I am a mathematician," Nicolaus offers.

"This is my son, Guntrum, who must begin to think of his future."

"Guntrum," WERNER asks, "do you like philosophy or mathematics, or perhaps carving, like your father?"

The boy is too shy to answer, so his father responds, "He is the oldest of my eight children and shows talent for carving. When I finish Casimir's tomb, I think we shall all return to Nuremberg."

"Maybe you can leave Guntrum here to study or to decorate another church for us," WERNER persists. "I have to admit my mind wandered during the funeral. I counted eighteen angels that embellish your altar-piece, and I was thinking that should be enough to lift the darkest soul to heaven."

"Or that big family of Jagellos," Stoss retorts. "If you will excuse me, I must return inside to make a few more sketches for the tomb."

"What is your plan," Nicolaus inquires, "carved wood, painted or plain?"

110

"It is to be of red marble, an interesting challenge for me." Veit and his son return to the Cathedral.

"We should get to class," Nicolaus comments.

"Are you still so intrigued with the perspective class?" WERNER asks.

"Not at all. Once the geometry is clear, it isn't very exciting. Optics is what really fascinates me." Copernicus stops. "How can we be talking of art and science when we have just seen our dead King?"

WERNER contemplates that question. Krakow University is almost 100 years old; its curriculum reflects the spirit of humanism. Students there are being taught to reconcile the philosophy of the ancient Greeks and Romans to a belief in one God. Mental sorting through Plato and Aristotle have given WERNER an answer.

"Perhaps it is Aristotle's Golden Mean, all things in moderation. After a funeral, people need to talk of living."

"My father died when I was young," Copernicus states. "He was Polish, of course, and lived his whole life under Casimir's rule. My German mother wanted to return to her people. I wonder how long I will live?"

"My friend," WERNER replies, "only God knows. Think on living. Since the Church is your guardian, and you are such an outstanding mind, you may be invited to teach and continue your studies in Rome."

22nd day of Rabi I, 897 A.H.

Bayazid II is a man of culture and intellect. Within the walls of the Topkapi Palace, he enjoys the treasures acquired in the conquests that began with Osman I, who founded the Ottoman Empire 100 years ago. Today, his territory stretches south to Athens, east to the border of Persia, across the Black Sea to the north to the Crimea, and west to Romania.

This morning the Sultan receives visitors with gifts. The representative from Azerbaijan brings furs, from Kurdistan come carpets, and from Bulgaria jars of sweet syrup. All the ambassadors look quite elegant in robes of velvet, satin and silver brocade. They have been loaned robes from the palace storeroom for the occasion. Bayazid greets each man and inspects the tribute. He learns that the syrup comes from a tree sap and is as sweet as honey. He thanks the visitor but notes privately the ugliness of the ceramic jars. The carpets are truly lovely. One carpet entirely of silk has an unusual turquoise blue which is accented with tiny white chevrons; another cotton prayer rug has the mihrab shape just like the niche in a mosque that faces towards Mecca. Bayazid is most attracted to a large wool carpet gleaming with earthy shades of warm browns and reds, contrasted with deep blue, and accented with peach and lemon yellow in geometric designs. At the Sultan's request, the carpet is lifted so he can inspect the tiny hand tied knots and the velvety front.

"Both sides are beautiful," he comments, "but will the colors stay as strong?"

112

"Yes, master," replies the Kurdistani, "for our alchemists always test the dyes and are doubly careful to use only proven colors for anything we present to you."

The sable furs do not inspire much enthusiasm on a warm June day, and the representatives are dismissed.

The Sultan strolls in his garden where a few tulips are still blooming in shady places. Outside he can hear the mid-day call to prayer from the minarets at the mosque. Istanbul, the capital of the Ottoman Empire, is mainly the work of his father Mohammed II, who conquered the Byzantine capital of Constantinople in 1453, changed its name and its famous church. Inside Saint Sofia, he had the mosaics plastered over and added a mihrab, a simple niche facing Mecca. The 900 year old Roman Catholic church was built with some ancient marble pillars from the temple of Diana at Ephesus; now the exterior has received four tall slender minarets that actually complement the huge domed structure. Close by, Mohammed II built his Topkapi Palace at the corner of two great waterways, the Bosporus and the Golden Horn.

Bayazid likes to remember his father from the portraits painted by Gentile Bellini of Venice. In one, Mohammed II is seated cross-legged. A red and white turban tops his sensitive bearded face. His right hand, with a ring on his thumb and on his little finger, holds a rose near his long and elegant nose. Another shows Mohammed's face framed by a sumptuous arch and six crowns. Bayazid was in his twenties when Bellini came, and remembers him also for the erotic paintings he made for his father, the forty-nine-year-old Sultan. Bayazid didn't see them at the time. Two years later, with Gentile Bellini gone and his father dead, Bayazid discovered these stimulating paintings. He wondered if the artist had been admitted to the Seraglio.

Mohamet II by Gentile Bellini.
Reproduced by courtesy, the Trustees of the National Gallery, London.

Wives must be treated equally and with respect. The concubines of the harem were probably the models.

Returning from the garden to dine with the Sultana is the usual mid-day routine for the ten years he has ruled. They eat artichoke hearts and spicy lamb, and sip peach juice. This food is served on the elegant grey-green celadon ware from China, because tradition holds that it will detect poison in the food by changing color. Bayazid admires fine ceramics and has directed that some of the crates that were stored in unused sections of the Topkapi Palace be opened. He delights in the pure white bone porcelain with charming scenes in vivid blue from Ming China. Melon slices and grapes are served on these dishes accompanied by a syrupy nut-filled cookie and hot tea.

"What are your thoughts?" asks the Sultana.

"I was thinking of Venice this morning," he replies. "The Venetians made treaties with the Persians against us, but after my father defeated them both, he invited Venice to send him a painter. They sent Gentile Bellini, a man about his same age. I wonder if he is still alive? We have been at peace, but now the Venetians are threatening me again from their new location in Cyprus."

"Those Christians seem to provoke wars and battles," she responds.

"My dear, if only it were just the Christians! Our Islamic brothers in Persia conspired with them, and you know the troubles I have had with the Mamelukes. Perhaps as Shiite Moslems, they feel justified in engaging in a Holy War against their own."

The Sultana reacts, "But we Sunnites accept all the first four caliphs after Mohammed, while they deny the first three. We have the true faith."

Without answering her, Bayazid signals to his servants that the meal is ended. Let his wife return to the Seraglio

115

and their three young sons. Corcud, Ahmed, and Selim are fine boys, but he worries that their mother is encouraging them to be warlike.[18]

After an afternoon of interviews with his naval commanders and the pleasures of his harem, Bayazid listens to a financial review of Empire expenses. The *sutfaya*, bill of exchange, makes trading less cumbersome, but the use in the last few years of + and - makes the Sultan more assured that his questions could penetrate even the tricks of mathematicians.

For the evening, he orders musicians to play on a northern porch overlooking the water. The lute sets the melody; the tambour drum keeps a rhythmic beat. The singers are loud, and enthusiastically accompany themselves with syncopated clapping. Bayazid invites his oldest son, Corcud, to join him. He thinks, "I suppose I should tell him about his grandfather who built the castle north of here at the narrowest part of the Bosporus to control these waters. But I would hate to tell him of the slaughter when our armies defeated the Byzantines at this very spot with big cannons built for us by Urban of Hungary."

Instead he signals the musicians to sing more quietly and says, "Corcud, come stand by me and look at the sea. This Bosporus joins the Aegean to the Black Sea. From here we can watch many boats go by, and we can decide who will pass."

"Yes, father."

"And look to your left and see the large long bay there. It doesn't go to another sea, but stops like a long horn with two prongs. See how golden it looks as the sun sets behind it? That is why it is called the Golden Horn."

"When Constantine put an iron chain across the entrance, Grandfather Mohammed had his army carry

116

seventy boats overland to defeat him," Corcud says. "Mother taught me that!"

"Yes, son," the Sultan replies.

As the earth continues her steady rotation, the sun disappears below the horizon, and the Golden Horn isn't golden anymore.

National Day

A parade through the capital city will launch the celebration of National Day. Who can sleep in Reykjavik? Babies and old people, perhaps. But with a clear sunny day and a national holiday falling on a Sunday, there are better things to do. The sun will not set for several weeks but teases the horizon in the west side of north with a long glow of sunset which melts into a sunrise in the northeast.

GUNTER LEIFSON, fisherman and sheep raiser, and his wife, TILLE ERIKSDOTTIER, live in a sturdy house located near hot springs. The springs not only provide hot water, but heat for the building. GUNTER'S father, LEIF NILSSON lives with them, and his father NILS OLAFSON had helped him build this house. LEIF has offered to cook a holiday meal of sheep's head, blood sausage, and fresh cod to go with the greens from the garden while his grandchildren and their parents have an outing.

Ten-year-old Tor will hike with his parents, but two-year-old BERGOLITE will ride on her father's strong back. The childrens' names are TOR GUNTERSON and BERGOLITE GUNTERSDOTTIER. Like her mother, BERGOLITE will keep this name when she marries (her given name and her father's given name plus "dottier").

Their destination is toward Geysir, but it is a long walk. TOR prefers the speed of skis in winter. With the air temperature at a balmy 62 degrees, soon GUNTER needs to stop and remove his jacket. Their clothes are made by TILLE, who spins and weaves the wool from their Icelandic sheep, using the beiges and browns for accents on the white wool. GUNTER is happy to put BERGOLITE down for a while. She

118

is anxious to stretch her legs. Geysir is the site of many bubbling pools and steaming vents. Volcanic action has built this island in the Arctic, and those forces of nature continue to work. Suddenly, the most famous hot spring at Geysir sends a spout 195 feet into the air. There is time for everyone to get a good look.

Returning to their home, the family is greeted by a ruddy-faced Grandfather LEIF, who asks if they are hungry. TILLE is pleased that her father-in-law is such a help with cooking. She will prepare skyr, a yogurt-like dessert, and then change into her long black dress with gold embroidery.

On National Day, it is well to remind the children that Iceland has been governed by its own people for 562 years. The 60 members of the Althing are elected to an upper and lower house. Although Kings of Norway and Denmark have sometimes ruled here, it was by invitation of the Althing. Ninety years ago there were hardly enough people to serve, after the Black Death took its terrible toll. Iceland lost two-thirds of its people. In Europe, cities suffered such losses, but those fleeing to the countryside and the many who already lived in less density were better able to avoid the rat-carried plague. But farming is only one percent of the land use in Iceland. Fishing is the main occupation. Numerous coastal towns to the north have been abandoned because ice has clogged their harbors. It is definitely colder than when grandfather LEIF was a boy. Today's sunny warm weather is doubly appreciated.

After his family eats heartily, GUNTER reads the heroic sagas of Icelandic heroes. These stories are just 300 or 400 years old, young compared to the age of the Althing. Grandfather LEIF nods off before the story ends. BERGOLITE, cozy in his lap, looks up as his jaw slackens and his head bobbles. TILLE puts a finger to her lips to signal her daughter not to disturb his well deserved rest. BERGOLITE

119

complies and soon her eyelids begin to close and flutter and close. The Arctic sun continues to shine. Tor is still alert: he remembers the days of November and December when daylight lasts only two hours. He'll catch up on his sleep then.

Deep in equatorial Africa, goats, pigs and cattle are tethered among the palm trees. Paths between the straw houses wind to a large public area and royal buildings. In the jungle are leopards and civet cats; near the river, crocodiles, parrots, and herons.

The Bantu people are subjects of Mani Kongo, the absolute ruler of more than one million people. Mani Kongo's court, slaves, and harem entertain him with music and dance; he is carried in an elaborate litter. He controls six principalities because he can summon an army of 100,000 men in a matter of days. He also controls the cowrie shell monetary system. Different dialects of Bantu are spoken in his kingdom, but none has writing. There is no calendar. One day is much the same as the next in equatorial Africa.

Mani Kongo and his subjects wear copper jewelry, furs, and fabrics that appear to be velvet or printed cotton, but all are woven of raffia. That was until four years ago when Portuguese explorers brought gifts of cotton and wool fabric. The Europeans were amazed at the beauty of native fabrics but needed a bartering item so they could return with the prized elephant ivory. Rather than trade raw ivory, many skilled Africans already are carving Christian subjects and armed Portuguese on horses.

Just eight years ago, sailors from King John of Portugal had set two stone pillars at the mouth of the Congo River and sent emissaries inland with gifts. Then four years ago Bartolomio Dias de Novias sailed past the pillars at the port city of Mpenda to Mani Kongo's capital. Dias was returning from the first recorded trip around the southern tip of Africa, and he made a personal call on the king. He was cordially received. Mani Kongo had even sent emissaries, including his son Nsaku, to Lisbon.

Last year, the Portuguese returned with news. Nsaku had been baptized a Christian, taking the name of João da Silva, John of the Woods. Unfortunately, he and the others have died of the plague on the return voyage. The sixty-year-old monarch hears of his son's experience and the claims of Christianity and accepts baptism and a new name. Named Nzinga a Nkuwu at birth, he was given the royal title, Mani Kongo, by his father. At baptism, the royal family of the Congo became John, Eleanor, and Alfonso, the prince, in honor of the royal family of Portugal. Mani Kongo/John accepted a banner from Pope Innocent VIII, and mobilized his people to build a large church in just two months. When some of his subjects rebelled at this European intrusion, then Mani Kongo's army put them to route.

In June 1492, however, the Christian Congo leader is dealing with pressures to change his polygamous lifestyle and the whole social order of his kingdom. The beautiful bronze statues, some hundreds of years old, that have stood for authority for centuries, seem to be losing their power. One son, who has refused baptism and is enjoying the pleasures of his father's harem, provides a rallying point for local autonomy and keeping to the old ways.

Wednesday

A month has past since Colón read the orders from the King and Queen, but they have not been acted upon. The only official response to this date has been an order drafted by Juan de Coloma suspending criminal proceedings against any man who would be willing to go. The mayor's response has been one that is typical in Spain, "The orders were obeyed, but they have not been acted upon." Independence and defiance in small Spanish towns avoid confrontation. Fernando and Isabella have sent further orders to Juan de Pinalosa. They want prompt action.

The Pinzón brothers own a part interest in a caravel named the Pinta. Martin Pinzón is willing to add this ship to the two royal ships for a 1/8 interest in Colón's 10% of the gold and spices they return to Spain. Further, Martin Pinzón will recruit good sailors, he wants no jail birds on this voyage. Colón agrees; at last plans begin in earnest.

123

Thursday

Little Prince Henry is one year old. Of course he is named for his father, Henry VII, King of England, but his older brother, Arthur is the heir. With all the killing that ended the struggles between the houses of Lancaster and York, the King knows that, although their mother is Elizabeth of York, his sons will have to gain backing from both houses for the new Tudor dynasty to continue. Thus, "Arthur", a name of wisdom and strength in ancient English lore, is chosen for the first born. The Caxton Press at Westminster published *Le Morte d'Arthur* eight years ago. Royalty and some monasteries had hand-made copies of Sir Thomas Malory's poetic prose, but printing made it available to gentlefolk. With a name like Arthur, the prince should capture the imagination and loyalty of the English.

Elizabeth is glad her mother lived to know the baby Henry. The queen mother died June 8, and little Margaret and Arthur cannot understand why she is absent. Little Henry should make a fine churchman, his parents think. He certainly is a ruddy, healthy toddler.

Another one year old is Inigo Lopez de Racalde. Born and living in the Basque country of northern Spain, his noble family plans a military career for him; in a few years he will go as a page to the court of Isabella and Fernando.

The future of these two seems assured, but many things change. Who would think that Henry, destined as a second son for holy orders, would be called upon to marry the widow of his brother Arthur, Catherine of Aragon? He, called to rule England, would break with the Pope and establish the Church of England. Who would imagine that little Inigo, a page to Isabella, Fernando and their daughter, the same Catherine of Aragon, would, as a gallant courtier, be wounded and read with profound interest *The Life of Christ and Flowers of the Saints*? This child from the castle of Loyola in the Basque region will take Holy Orders as Ignatius Loyola and will found the Jesuit Order and be canonized a saint.

In nearby Navarre, a baby girl, Marguerite, was "born smiling and held out her little hand to each comer".[19] She was not named for the marguerite daisy, but for the Latin word for pearl. Her mother, Louise of Saxony, wishing to conceive, had swallowed a pearl to increase her hopes for pregnancy. With such a romantic beginning, is it any wonder Marguerite became a poet and patron of the arts as well as Queen of Navarre.

Friday

The candles burn low, and Alex and Yelena are fighting again.

"You've had enough wine, Alex," Yelena's hand reaches to snatch the carafe before her husband grabs it to fill his glass again.

"How dare you tell me what to do!" Alex stands, somewhat unsteadily. "Give me that wine."

Yelena soothingly says, "My dear, I know you are sad about your father's death, but..."

"My father rot in hell!" Alex yells, "Give me my wine." He grabs the wine and with a brutal shove sends Yelena crashing to the floor.

"You monster, you've hurt me."

Alex starts to kick her, but the sight of his oldest servant standing in the shadows changes his mood. The Grand Duke of Lithuania, Alexander I, pours himself another glass of wine and orders, "BASIL, bring me some sausage and cabbage, and bring some for the Duchess also."

BASIL leaves for the kitchen, not daring to help Yelena to her feet.

When Alexander's father, Casimir IV died, his older brother John Albert became King of Poland and Alexander inherited Lithuania. In both territories, the landed gentry are pushing for more power. With so many landless peasants, why should one family reap all the benefits from their exploitation? Power breeds brutality in some, and loss of power, frustration and despair.

"Your father is the cause of my troubles," Alexander shouts at Yelena. "It's not my father's death, it's your father stirring up the Jews against me and sending his troops across our borders."

Yelena, daughter of Ivan the Great of Russia, sits on the floor in the shadows but does not answer.

"Your father has no regard for you or me." Another glass of wine and Alexander is feeling sorry for himself. "He forces me to sign his treaty, recognizing him as Tsar of All Russians, to keep his soldiers from my door. Has he outgrown Moscow?"

Yelena knows her father is ambitious. He will win, sometimes with the sword and sometimes with the swordless hand of diplomacy. Ivan arranged for her brother to wed the Moldavian princess to surround Poland, and it is thanks to her father that she is in this loveless marriage. Yelena winces, as putting weight on her right hand causes a sharp pain in her shoulder, but she rises to her feet. She is the daughter of the Tsar and a Byzantine Princess. Like her mother, she is beautiful and strong. The Duchess of Lithuania will not let Alexander see her pain. Her loyalty is to herself, to the people, and to her father.

What a mistake it was to take Alexander's wine! Let him drink and forget. She makes a little curtsy. "Good night," she says flatly and turns, takes a candle, and leaves him in the increasing darkness.

July

Sunday

The Bellini family has grown up with art. Papa Jacopo Bellini had established his reputation as a prominent painter of Venice. After his death at age 70 in 1470, his sons, Gentile and Giovanni carried the name to further prominence. Their sister, Nicolosia, married Andrea Mantegna, and posed for him and her brothers. Now all three painters are in their early 60's and seem to have kept their good health along with the joy in their work.

They are assembling at Gentile's home for Sunday dinner. The Mantegnas arrive, followed by Giovanni and his student, Tiziano Vecelli.[20] After some polite greetings, Gentile asks, "Tiziano, have you ever seen the Festa della Sena?"

"No, sir. What is it?"

"Our Doge, Agostina Barbarigo, takes his royal boat and rides out the Grand Canal toward the long Lido Island. When he comes to the lagoon of San Nicolo where the Adriatic Sea begins, he marries Venice to the sea." Giovanni realizes that his description is not very clear and adds, "Oh, you should go see for yourself."

"Yes," Nicolosia urges, "there is time before dinner. You won't be able to see the ceremony where the Doge tosses the gold ring into the lagoon, but he should be coming back to his palace soon. Go there. Everyone follows him in decorated boats. It's quite a pageant."

"If you will all excuse me, I will go," the fifteen-year-old apprentice replies.

"Certainly," the old timers nod. Tiziano gets his hat, grabs for sketching paper and charcoal, and departs.

Time flies as the artists talk shop. Giovanni continues to be excited about oil paints. "I can get such depth and mystery by layering the oils. I think my apprentice is already showing great promise in oils."

"I still prefer the old tempera paint," Gentile Bellini comments. "It dries more quickly and gives sharp contrast for detail. I just grind my lapis lazuli for a brilliant blue, or my ochers for an orangy yellow, mix with egg yolk and water, and I'm ready to paint."

"It's the same with oils," Giovanni counters, "I mix my lapis with oil, the preparation is almost the same. But when I underpaint a skin area green and then gradually add pinks and creamy whites, the thin pinks give a life-like brown shadow where it barely covers the green."

"Well, we all change," Mantegna interjects. "Those huge frescoes I used to do. What a lot of work adding color to wet plaster, and there was no chance to correct a mistake. Plaster dries so quickly."

Gentile Bellini's memories of his time in Istanbul are still vivid. Sent to the Court of Mohammed II in 1479 as a court painter, he has a clear memory of the ambition and power of the Ottoman ruler. When he returned to Venice, he had a new appreciation of home, Venice the beautiful empire on the Adriatic Sea. He wonders if the sunlight and opulence have softened the Doge, so he does not realize the extent of the Ottoman threat. Sultans were aggressive and ruthless. After Gentile had painted portraits and erotica for his Turkish patron, he started a Christian scene, the beheading of John the Baptist. Mohammed II, found fault with the realism and had a slave decapitated before his eyes. The brutality of the Ottoman court was a more vivid memory for Gentile than their high aesthetic standards.

The apprentice returns.

"It was quite a sight," Tiziano volunteers. "You should have come."

"We have seen it often," his teacher responds, "but this time we would rather hear your impressions."

"All the boats were quite wonderful, barges and gondolas, but the Bucintoro, the Doge's ship of state, is really a sight to see." The boy continues, "The Doge rides in a tall sort of castle at the front. It is all carved with San Marco's lion and great Neptunes with tridents, and painted red and gold. There must be 30 oarsmen on each side, so it moves with great speed. I tried to sketch, but it was hard to get the perspective." The apprentice shows his sketch.

"It looks lovely, dear," Nicolosia comments after a quick glance.

"What's this?" Giovanni puts his finger at the bottom of the sketch.

"Sir, it is the Bucintoro," Tiziano replies.

"I can recognize that; but what is at the water line?"

"The thirty oars rowing as one. I couldn't figure out how to show it."

"My boy, the line is beautiful, especially the Neptunes; you have done well with shading and highlights. Tomorrow, we will go to the Armory, where Venice has always built her ships. You shall sketch boats in dry dock and master the perspective," Giovanni directs.

"Yes, Master," Tiziano says. "Maybe someday I could paint this beautiful pageant."

"For that you must study with my brother, Gentile; he's the pageant painter in this family, and a very fine host, too."

6 Kan 0 Pop[22]

Preparations for the new year are underway in the land of the turkey and deer. New mats and pottery are being prepared, old debts are settled, new clothing woven and decorated. Pop, the first month of the Mayan calendar also means woven grass mat. The authority figure is the Hop Pop, he who sits at the head of the mat.

Xib and Caan are anxious to go to Dzibichaltun to celebrate the new year. Caan has been making pottery as her people have for 3500 years. She rolls coils of clay, and pats and shapes the vessels until they are smooth and ready for firing. The priest said this is an auspicious day for pottery firing. Caan is 18 years old, 4'8" with long black straight hair, chestnut skin, and lovely white teeth filed to a point. She doesn't have jade inlaid in her teeth, but her mother does.

When Caan and Xib were married four years ago, family and friends helped them build their simple house of stone and mud walls with a thatched roof. Two papaya trees grow at the door and nearby they grow corn, squash and beans on mats floating in the swamp. Today, Xib is hunting. Perhaps he will kill a deer or, at least, a turkey to prepare for the great new year's celebration. More importantly, he must pay his debts to begin the year successfully. A deer would be a big help at this festival time. He might use its hide and meat as direct payment, or take it to the city to trade for cocoa beans, which serve as Mayan money. If hunting is poor, they may sell Caan's pottery.

Game is scarce. X<small>IB</small> has heard his father and grandfather tell of the tall trees and the pheasants, turkeys, jaguars, and deer they had hunted in their youth. But the great storm[23] had come with such force and continued from evening to noon the next day, killing animals, uprooting forests, destroying homes, and even toppling tall temples. It seemed a final blow to a people who had built wondrous stone cities of pyramids, temples and ball courts, but had abandoned them when food ran short or enemies threatened.

X<small>IB</small> is proud that his birth could be remembered by the great storm. Not that life was something to be grasped. It was natural and death was natural. One might offer his life, to jump in the *cenote*, sacred well, to ask the rain god for rain. His life might have ended the same night he was born, because of the great storm. It was recorded in the books he loved to read. His people recorded the life of the court, the special celebrations each 52 years when the old temples are burnt, and new ones constructed over them. The elaborate and accurate Mayan calendar and books serve as a framework for their lives and predictors of good or bad days ahead. These books are written on long papers folded accordion style and encased in wood. When they become tattered with years of use, they are lovingly recopied.[24]

X<small>IB</small> thought his mother was quite remarkable to survive that stormy night, when thousands died, and to care for him. Their house was flattened, but she took her children to a nearby cave to wait out the storm, and there he was born. X<small>IB</small> admired his mother for her courage and strength. He rarely thought of the months she carefully bound his head between two boards to produce his broad elongated forehead, because all Mayan mothers of good families did that. It is strange that he is not a father after being married for four years.

The hunter reminds himself to look for signs of the deer he needs rather than dream of his lovely wife and the books he has seen. In loin cloth and sandals, he moves quietly through the tropical forest; he is the same height as his wife, 4'8", but certainly more muscular. A rustle above him alerts him to a wild turkey. Silently XIB strings his bow and places the arrow he has so carefully straightened and decorated with feathers. But the wily old turkey gives a gobble and starts an awkward flight. XIB's arrow grazes a wing, and the large bird veers and struggles, but continues to flee, dropping to the ground to better use its strong legs. Quickly XIB runs after it; another arrow is already in place. This one stops the turkey's escape, but the big bird continues to thrash. XIB grabs his stone knife and cuts its throat. Then he uses his knife to cut his own penis to shed a few drops of blood. The hunter always offers blood for blood, and XIB disliked cutting his tongue, the other accepted member, because he could not see his incision. A blood offering thanks the gods for providing food, and reminds the hunter that killing for sport is not acceptable.

Because of the new year debts, XIB should continue to hunt. A turkey is not a deer. But he decides to go home early. He will surprise CAAN.

XIB calls out to his wife as he enters his house. A moan comes from the blankets in the corner.

"I will kill you," he shouts. "I will crush your head with a stone."

"No, no," CAAN pleads, "there is no man here with me. I am true to you. I am feeling sick."

The husband's suspicions are correct but his timing is slow. He may kill his wife for adultery, but only if he catches her in the act.

"Are you too sick to go to Dzibichaltun for the new year?" he asks.

"I don't know."

"Why don't you urinate in your sandal and drink it? That cured me last year." XIB offers a Mayan remedy.

"I'll try the powdered deer horn first."

CAAN is fine in the morning, and wears her nose ring, ear rings, perfume and a *huipile* she has woven. XIB brings his stilts for a special new year's dance. Miles of old stone roadways make it possible for the people to gather for the celebration. The *cuxan san*, roadways suspended in the sky, go to the old abandoned city of Coba and to the coast at Xelha, where other Mayans use 80 foot canoes carved from a single cedar tree to harpoon fish and manatees. The jungle is beginning to cover the road to Chichen Itza. Its pyramid and temple with 1000 columns have been abandoned for almost 300 years. The seven ball courts are overgrown by jungle. Only Dzibichaltun remains as a major city.

The Quiche Mayans gather to launch the new year. There is buying, selling and trading. A slave may be bought for one cocoa bean. One hundred and fifty women form a circle for the dance of the reeds. They toss the reeds to each other like jugglers. Dancers wear bells of copper, gold and silver; flutes and conch shells add melody to the rhythm of the rattles and great variety of drums. Some ceramic drums are as tall as a man and covered with deer intestines. The men perform a shield dance and a monkey dance, as well as the skillful dance on stilts. On platforms, humorous plays are performed with costumes and masks.

Afternoon rain showers begin, and soon soak everyone's new clothing and mats. CAAN and XIB will spend

135

the night with relatives before returning home. An afternoon and night of heavy rain is common at this time of year, and welcome for filling the *cenotes* and watering the beans and corn. Some years have been plagued by drought.

The older Mayans remember when they celebrated Pop, the first month of the eighteen month year, in the great walled city of Mayapan. It has been abandoned for fifty years. Its kings lie buried in stone tombs. The observatory and temples with carved stone decorations and fresco paintings are being covered by jungle. When the fierce Itzas from the west attacked, even Kukulcan, the Mayan feathered serpent god, could not save them.

Mayans believe that there are no accidents. If a man is careless and knocks over his neighbor's bee hive, he is judged and punished, the same as one who willfully destroys the property. They accept the defeat of Mayapan and do not strive to reclaim it. The trance inducing plants, used for centuries to make their system of human sacrifice more palatable, continue to foster a sense of well being while their once great culture slips from its former grandeur.

Monday

The brothers of San Spirito provide a home for Michelangelo Bounarroti, striking in contrast to his surroundings of a few months ago. With the death of his patron, Michelangelo has had to leave the villa and gardens of the great Lorenzo de Medici. The tiny monk's cell he now occupies is unadorned save for his cherished sculpture of the Battle of the Lapiths and Centaurs; the food is simple but adequate.

Michelangelo sketches because he cannot carve; there is neither room nor material available. He makes small models to serve as a guide when he can again drive his chisel into marble. The monks are sympathetic, not only to the patients at San Spirito Hospital, but to the young artist. They allow him to improve his craft by studying and dissecting the cast-off bodies of those whose souls have gone to heaven.

The weight of a lifeless body when the muscles no longer respond to the brain's commands, and the details of the skeleton, veins and muscle are revealed to him, as well as how the skin covers them all. The hospital is not as pleasant a place to work as was Lorenzo's sculpture garden, where the young artist copied antique Roman statues while Bertoldo offered advice, but here the lessons are profound. A crucified Christ on the cross or a dead Christ in his mother's arms must show the physical reality of death and the hope of eternal life. Here among the merciful brothers, Michelangelo learns both.

Winter

A family of four walks through the arid land of central Australia accompanied by their four dingoes. TINTARA, the man, carries a spear, spear-thrower, boomerang, and fire-stick in his brown hand. His thick black hair and beard top his slender, tall body, clad only in a loin cloth. NUMA, his woman, carries her digging stick and balances a large wooden bowl on her head. It contains a few wooden dishes, some stone implements, and a few seeds for eating, not planting. Two boys, ages 8 and 3 lag behind. Unlike their dark-haired mother, NUMA, the boys have bright yellow hair. It will darken as they mature. The same sun that bronzes their skin, bleaches their hair.

These nomadic people have no more belongings than they carry. They hunt and gather their food and have no shelters. The whole world is home. They know every tree, bush and rock, every spring and stream bed. TINTARA observes and shows the older boy the natural features that will take them nearer to the rock paintings.

The short days of winter are often sunny and pleasant. The family stops in mid-afternoon. Their four dogs, who have been ranging widely to hunt during the journey, arrive to check this night's site. TINTARA directs the boys to a dry stream bed, and they begin to dig for water. NUMA removes the wooden bowl from her head. Her eyes scan the land in every direction and observe the smallest detail.

TINTARA comes to her side and asks, "Do you see any signs of emu?"

"No, but there may be quail in those bushes."

138

Numa has located a place where yams should grow. Though she has walked 8 miles today, she takes her digging stick and walks another mile to dig wild yams.

While the boys continue to dig with their hands for water, Tintara gathers a few dry leaves and twigs. By blowing on the ember in his fire stick, he soon has a small fire. The boys have reached some water at 2 feet. Tintara joins them to deepen the hole. The sandy earth settles to the bottom and each person and the four dingoes lap a refreshing drink.

"Boys, get more branches for the fire before it is dark," Tintara instructs. "It will be cold tonight."

Numa returns with six large yams and some extras, lily roots and a decaying piece of wood. The wood contains their first course, live termites and crunchy grubs. After getting a drink of water, Numa sits by the fire to prepare the food. Her younger son is in her lap as quick as a bandicoot and grabs her breast to nurse. At three, he should be weaned sometime soon, but there is contentment and rest for both of them for now.

A boomerang cuts through the air and brings down a quail, which Tintara has flushed from the bushes. He returns and puts it in the fire with the yams. Now he can relax. The western sky is a tongue color below the darkening clouds. Smoke from other fires is visible; other *yulngu*[25] are coming near to the hollow log totem for the longest night. It should be quite a gathering.

The other *yulngu* will be pleased to see how much the boys have grown. Tintara does not call himself their father, even though he and Numa have lived together for nine years. The elder is the son of eucalyptus totem, and the younger is the son of the spirit of dark grey boulder. Tintara does not associate sexual intercourse with the birth of his children. All believe they were fathered in Numa when she was near the powerful totem spirits.

After dinner, the fire is divided into four small fires. Numa keeps the younger child near her, and a dingo comes to provide additional warmth for their nude bodies. The older boy sleeps alone with a dingo, and Tintara has one dog at his back and one at his feet. Should it get any colder, a three dog night, the family might rearrange. The earth is their bed and the sky their covers.

In the morning, Numa grinds the seeds she has carried and makes little cakes which she cooks in the ashes. Cold yams and a drink of water complete the meal. The boys are encouraged to watch for larger game like emu or kangaroo because today they will join the other *yulngu*.

When the sun is directly above, they come to the painted rocks. The large white eyes of Lightning Brother dominate his undulating figure. The abstract body is painted on the rock in white lead oxide mixed with animal fat and ocher clay. The seven foot image is still taller than Tintara, who remembers being awed by Lightning Brother when he was a young boy. Now he repeats the story of the Dreamtime when every stone and lizard and bush were created.

Before continuing on their way, Numa shows some kookaburra eggs she found this morning. They eat them raw. Tintara's sharp eyes see the *yulngu* about two miles west. He also sees a kangaroo to the north.

"Numa, take my fire-stick and boomerang and go to the gathering. I will hunt and meet you there."

The boys are wide eyed as they near the group of fifty to sixty people. For the first time in months, they see other blonde children. Some of the men look like Lightning Brother. Using charcoal, lead oxides and clays, the men are painting their bodies to prepare for the dances.

140

Spontaneity is never discouraged. Some men imitate animals they have hunted. A painted body makes them feel like dancing. Some group dances last several days.

The women decorate their bodies, too. NUMA fixes her hair with orange clay and puts white bands on her arms and legs. Her boys beg to be decorated, too. The earliest form of painting in all the earth is body painting.

Meanwhile, TINTARA has been stalking a kangaroo. He is careful to stay down-wind of the animal and approach it silently and slowly. The unwary kangaroo hops and stops. Crouching, TINTARA puts the end of his spear shaft into the notch of the spear-thrower. As the kangaroo turns towards him, TINTARA stands and hurls the spear, felling the animal with one well planned throw. He looks at the bent stick in his hand. Without the spear-thrower, which acts like an extension of his arm, his pointed stick would not have had the force to pierce the kangaroo's hide. The dingoes come to lick the blood as the hunter completes the kill.

To transport the ninety pound kangaroo, TINTARA drags the animal over smooth ground and carries it across his shoulders through rocky terrain. His efforts are rewarded when the *yulngu* greet him with admiration and praise. A big fire is built. There will be a feast for all on the longest night.

TINTARA has the privilege of cooking the kangaroo in the traditional manner. Grabbing the animal by its large tail, he flings it into the fire!

141

Wednesday

"Giovanni Battista Cibó," the *Camerlengo*, Chamberlain, calls out as he lifts the linen cloth from the corpse's face. The dead man does not respond to his baptismal name. "Giovanni Battista Cibó," this time the *Camerlengo* taps the head with a silver hammer. After repeating the hammer taps and calling to "Innocent", it is time for an official announcement.

"The Pope is dead," the *Camerlengo* announces to the other Cardinals who accompany him. "Begin the *novemdiali.*" A series of nine masses will be said for the soul of the deceased.

Pope Innocent VIII!'s fisherman's ring is removed from his stiff, white hand. The ring contains a cameo of Saint Peter with a fishing net. The Papal seal is brought, and the *Camerlengo* destroys ring and seal with harder blows than he used on Innocent's head.

"The Secretary of State no longer serves," he announces. "No decrees will be issued."

When the Pope is buried in three days, the Cardinals will convene to elect a successor. Innocent was a handsome, likable, lax, Genoese, who died at the age of sixty. The first Pope to publicly recognize his children, he celebrated their marriages at the Vatican and often dined with ladies. His children were sired before he took Holy Orders, so while he apparently kept his vow of celibacy, his lifestyle encouraged a libertine atmosphere. As Cardinals lived openly with mistresses and pursued wealth for themselves and their children, the general population of Rome had also deteriorated into a lawless society.

142

Robbery, murder, rape and assault continued to increase during Innocent's eight year reign.

"Where is Djem?" Cardinal Giuliano della Rovere asks.

"I have seen that he is safe," Cardinal Rodrigo Borgia speaks with authority. The Cardinals may come to blows over this legacy of Innocent's reign. Djem, brother of the Ottoman ruler Bayazid II, is the hostage of the Pope. Ten years ago, Djem challenged his brother for the Ottoman throne, lost and fled to the island of Rhodes, a stronghold of the Crusader Knights of St. John. Bayazid paid the Knights 45,000 ducats[26] a year to keep Djem away. Djem was moved from Rhodes to the French estate of d'Aubusson, leader of the Knights of St. John. Pope Innocent gained control of this hostage by outbidding Isabella and Fernando, Ferrante of Naples, and even the Mameluke Sultan of Cairo. He was the only bidder who could offer a Cardinal's appointment as well as money. Bayazid's willingness to pay support made Djem a valuable hostage, financially and politically.

Innocent began his rule by sending the Inquisition to Germany to discover and destroy witches. At his death, he leaves his Grand Turk hostage, children and grandchildren, and the Belvedere Palace. His worldly lifestyle has touched education. Agostino Nifo is publishing a treatise proving that there are two kinds of truth, religious and philosophical. Also, at the University of Padua, Nicoletto Vernias is teaching that the world soul is immortal, not the individual soul. The body of Giovanni Battista Cibó is being washed and dressed in a white gown. What is the state of his soul?

Tuesday

"Painting is the superior art," thinks Leonardo, the sculptor, engineer, city planner, and architect, as his brush applies the underpainting for the *Virgin of the Rocks*. The basic composition is emerging, the craggy rocks in the wood panel's arched top above the triangle of characters with Mary's head at the apex, the infant John the Baptist at her right, and the Christ Child with an attending angel at her left.

The angel occupies Leonardo's thoughts for the moment. Almost twenty-five years ago, he painted an angel for his teacher, Verrocchio, a child-like angel full of awe and wonder. This angel extends a protective arm around the infant Jesus, just as Mary extends her right arm around his cousin John. Leonardo works quickly for a change, for the whole painting is a repetition of a work commissioned ten years ago when he first came to Milan. Now the Confraternity of the Immaculate Conception wants a new version. The brothers haven't told him what they have done with the first painting; perhaps they've given it to a benefactor or sold it to the highest bidder.

"Jachomo! keep grinding the golden ochres," Leonardo scolds his young apprentice and companion. "If you want me to buy you fine clothing and jewelry, I must complete this painting so I can get paid."

Leonardo wipes his brush, dips it in turpentine, and steps back to view his progress. He wipes his brow; the mid-day heat is beginning to penetrate his quarters in Sforza castle. Duke Ludovico continues to pressure him. Leonardo began this year directing the Duke's elaborate

144

wedding, then he designed ceiling decorations for this fortress-palace. Now that the bride is great with child, Ludovico wants the equestrian statue of his father completed. The future of the Sforza dynasty rests with this infant.

The artist continues his underpainting, outlining and laying in the lights and darks. Although Leonardo da Vinci is almost six feet tall, this panel bests him by a few inches, so he stands and paces before it. He sees that it is already becoming a window into the sacred scene. Jachomo has deserted his grinding and is looking at the sketches Leonardo made for the original painting. "You forgot to make the angel point its finger," the thirteen-year old chides.

"You're right," Leonardo says and thumbs through his sketches for the gentle Mary and the mysterious rocks, seeing evidence of his other preoccupations as well, designs for armaments, catapults, a tank and an air-screw (helicopter). "This time I won't paint so many flowers in the foreground either. It's too hot to think of spring flowers. Come, Jachomo, it's time for food and wine, and the undercoat can dry a bit while we nap."

Virgin of the Rocks by Leonardo da Vinci.
Reproduced by courtesy, the Trustees of the National Gallery, London.

August

12th day of Ab, 4252

Fernando is King of Sicily, Castile, and Aragon so his Edict of Exile applies to the Jews in all these places. In Sicily, 6,300 homes have been confiscated, and 40,000 Jews are leaving. Many are fleeing to Naples where Fernando's cousin, Ferrante I, is King.

The last of 200,000 Spanish Jews are crowding into port cities. From Cadiz on the Atlantic Ocean, some are heading to northern Europe. Poland welcomes Jews, but Lithuania doesn't. Perhaps they will find a home in London, Paris, or Amsterdam. Many scholars and mathematicians must leave their libraries, for boat captains have strict limits on baggage.

Many have left from Barcelona on the Mediterranean to join relatives who live in the Ottoman Empire. The Mameluke Sultanate in Cairo also welcomes Jews.

To stay in any Spanish territory, a Jew must convert to Christianity and be baptized. Then he must be prepared to answer to Torquemada the Inquisitor and prove that his conversion is real.

Thursday

Five ships are preparing to leave Palos this evening. Two boats loaded with exiled Jews will have a short trip to northern Africa. Three ships of Cristóbal Colón are getting a final inspection and a year's provisions are being stowed. Colón commands the largest, the Santa Maria, renamed from the Mary Gallant to reflect her holy mission. Martin Alonzo Pinzón commands the Pinta: his pilot is his younger brother, Francisco. Another brother, Vincente Pinzón commands the Niña; it was owned by Pero Alonso Niño, who is its pilot on the voyage. Everyone is on board for the night. The total crew for the three ships is ninety; almost all are Spaniards from Palos. Another twenty-six people are officers of the King and their servants. Luis de Torres has come to act as a translator to the people they will find across the sea. Luis is a *converso*, a Spanish Jew who has converted to Christianity. His language skills include Hebrew, Arabic, and Chaldean. No women and no priests are sailing.

Each caravel is armed with cannons, and their stone and lead shot also serves as ballast. They carry gifts of beads, mirrors, pins and needles, and bonnets. Colón also has letters from Fernando and Isabella to the Great Khan of Cathay and the Emperor of Japan with a blank place to insert the proper names. The gifts seem more appropriate to a less advanced civilization. Colón's contract has specified that he be governor of all lands he finds. Certainly his three small ships will be in no position to challenge the old empires of the Orient.

149

Departure of Columbus From Palos in 1492 by Emanuel Leutze.
Painted in 1855, oil on canvas 48" x 72". ©1990 New American Crossings, Inc. Used by permission.

Friday

One hour before sunrise, the Santa Maria begins to set her sails. She is 117 feet long with a main deck 66 feet long. Her square sails, decorated with crosses, are a signal to the Niña and the Pinta that it is time to go. The three ships sail down the Rio Tinto and join the ocean to catch this morning's outgoing tide to speed them on their way. The ships are heading west when the sun rises behind them.

Wednesday

The bathhouses of Basel are a social institution. If Albrecht Dürer had simply wanted to get clean, the Rhine River was right there. In Nuremberg, he had only seen the inside of two of the nineteen public bathhouses. In Basel, the young journeyman artist wants to visit every one. The university students gather to soak in warm waters, to drink and eat, to read and dispute, and to play the flute or lyre, or simply listen. Since many baths do not separate the sexes, prostitution flourishes in several. Albrecht enjoys all the activities plus observing and sketching the nude bodies that surround him.

Today he has brought a copy of the *Letters of Saint Jerome*, a book which has just been published by Nicolaus Kessler. This is the second edition for Kessler, a printer of Basel, but the first use of Dürer's woodcut as an impressive frontespiece. The popularity and influence of Saint Jerome with university students extend throughout Europe. The fourth century saint was a scholar who translated the Bible from Hebrew and Greek into Latin, and also wrote commentaries and letters. He traveled from Rome to Constantinople to Jerusalem, but also spent time as a hermit in the desert, an ascetic as well as a scholar.

Albrecht's woodcut shows St. Jerome pulling a thorn from the lion's paw, but the grateful lion has shown up in Jerome's home. The saint takes time from his translation of Genesis. The students should recognize the Latin, Greek and Hebrew letters in the three open books. Will they realize that Jerome had scrolls, not books, and that this curtained feather bed in the corner and the charming houses and hills seen through the door are Basel, not Jerusalem? The wealth of detail Dürer has included marks him as a master artist, but not a historian. Although he is still technically a journeyman, he is accepted by the printers as the finest woodblock carver in Basel. He has not carved his initials on the front, but written "Albrecht Dürer von Normergk" on the back. The students accept him as a friend and congratulate him on being published.

Saint Jerome has been called the forerunner of Desiderius Erasmus, the Dutch scholar who has just been ordained a priest at age twenty-five. Another Basel printer, Froben, will publish the essays and letters of Erasmus. Dürer will admire his witty writings, paint his portrait, and agree with his dedication to reforming the Church while preserving its unity. The admiration goes two ways. Erasmus will write, "Although Dürer is a marvel in all forms of art, what is truly remarkable is what he manages to convey without the use of color...There are just light, shade and depth, so that what the eye beholds seems to take on an added dimension...he draws phenomena such as fire, rays of light, thunder and lightning, banks of clouds. Thoughts and feelings, even the human soul are portrayed through physical attitudes...and all this in black and white; indeed it would be sacrilege to add color."[27]

Saint Jerome by Albrecht Dürer. Woodcut used as frontispiece for
Letters of Saint Jerome, Second Edition, Basel 1492.
Courtesy of the Library of Congress.

Thursday

Six days at sea and the Niña, Pinta and Santa Maria have found land.

"Here we are in Cathay," the pilot of the Santa Maria, Juan de la Cosa teases the passengers from the court. The sailors are not fooled. Some of them have sailed to Africa before, and recognized the south-west course to the Canary Islands.

The Pinta needs repairs. While Martin Pinzón's ship limps into port, the Niña and the Santa Maria visit the beautiful beaches of the Canary Islands. It is almost always warm and sunny here, so near the equator. But the Spaniards are not vacationing. They are looking for a boat to replace the Pinta, and continuing the evaluations of their own vessels. No new ship is found.

155

Friday

Another uncomfortably hot day in Rome. Cardinals meeting to elect a Pope assemble in the chapel built by Sixtus IV, the Sistine Chapel. Two weeks of balloting and politicking are beginning to wear on the princes of the Church. Cardinal Giuliano de la Rovere leans back and studies the ceiling.[28] That dark blue ceiling painted with hundreds of stars, has some cracks in it. It should be replastered; German craftsmen do solid work. The chapel is not even 20 years old. It will need repainting soon.

French Cardinals want a fellow countryman on the Papal throne, but Italian churchmen are fearful that King Charles of France will try to use a French Papacy to aid his claims to Naples. As a compromise, the Cardinal from Spain gathers votes from those opposed to France and those opposed to Italy, from those who wish to be out of Rome and its heat and those he has bribed; Rodrigo Borgia is elected Pope by the required 2/3 vote.

Born near Valencia 61 1/2 years ago, Rodrigo is older than the recently deceased Pope Innocent. He is well acquainted with the Curia. He was a Cardinal at 25, thanks to his Uncle Alfonso who was his guardian and, as Pope Calixtus III, bestowed that honor upon him. Before he was 30, Rodrigo was a Papal Vice Chancellor.

Pope Alexander VI, as Rodrigo Borgia now titles himself, has served under six Popes, and in an age of ecclesiastical abuse, he may well be the most corrupt. His personal wealth is immense from benefices in Spain, Italy, and Hungary. He openly acknowledges his four children born to Vanozza Catanei. His twelve-year-old daughter,

Lucretia Borgia, is betrothed to a Spanish nobleman, but as Pope, Alexander hopes to find her a better match.

To the Cardinals, he pledges to bring peace among the Medicis, Sforzas, Estes, and Borgias. "We Christians must be united to fight the infidel Turks."

Saturday

The three Fugger brothers, Ulrich, 51, Joerg, 39, and Jacob, 33, have expanded their grandfather's weaving business in Bavaria into mining interests throughout Europe. Their investments involve travel and correspondence; it is unusual to find all three Fugger brothers in Augsberg. When Joerg was a young man of twenty-one, he had Giovanni Bellini paint his portrait when he was in Venice.[29] When Jacob was in Venice, he learned the double-entry accounting system. The youngest brother, Jacob, is the true capitalist and prime mover of the family. He might summarize:

Fugger Assets	Fugger Liabilities
Mercury mines in Spain	Loan to Innocent VIII
Offices in Ghent	Letter of credit from Lorenzo de Medici
Copper mines in Hungary	(These should be assets, but the deaths of
Rights to Maximillian's mines	the principals make their collection difficult)
Mining and smelting equipment	
180,000 Florins	
230,900 Ducats	

Another asset is Jacob's bride, Ursula Thuzo of Krakow. Even before his marriage, Jacob's business partnership with the Thuzo family had added their copper mines to Fugger interests, enabling him to corner the copper market and raise prices. He has increased the price of copper by 50% in ten years.

The Fuggers loan money to Princes and Popes. In return for rights to his iron and silver mines, Maximillian

158

is called their Imperial Counselor; the Fuggers advance him money for his army. The Fuggers are staunch Catholics and donate, but also loan, money to the Pope. They are influential in changing the belief that only Jews should collect interest on money loaned.

Some recent transactions:

Debits	Credits
Franz von Taxis, for postal services	Payment for copper roofing from Lodovico Sforza
Employee salaries and benefits	Payment for gold ore to jeweler in Florence
Custom tax to Henry VII for importing tin and copper	Payment for iron and copper sold to ship yards in Seville

Jacob Fugger's accounting skills give them an edge over their competitors. While their metals, weaving, and banking interests are broad, Jacob has found it economical to use the services of Franz von Taxis to send contracts, cash and letters of credit between offices. Taxis's couriers are expensive but honest and reliable. The Fuggers do not have to run everything to be the richest family in Europe. Ulrich is childless, as is the newly married Jacob.[30] Joerg's three-year-old, Raymond, is the future for the Fugger family.

Saturday

The Pinta has been taken aground to repair her keel. All the provisions and ballast have been removed, and Martin Pinzón is confident that the work can be completed in another ten days.

The leaders and men are eager to go, but at the same time are keenly aware that they are sailing into a great unknown and their equipment must be flawless. Vincente Yanez Pinzón, commander of the Niña has found that his ship is slower than the larger Santa Maria. He orders all the lateen sails removed from his ship and altered from three-cornered to square sails. That should increase her speed.

From his surf board NANAKOA can see the palace grounds. The wooden buildings with thatched roofs that house the king are only slightly larger than those of his people. NANAKOA's house has a small shrine to Laka, the goddess of the hula; the king has a *heiau*, a large open air temple with images of Ku and Kane and other gods and goddesses carved of wood and decorated with shells and feathers. Outrigger canoes rest in the natural harbor. The king's land is still kapu (taboo), but adjoining it is a bit of shoreline called the City of Refuge.

Those who break a *kapu* are killed by stoning, being strangled or buried alive, but they will be spared if they reached the City of Refuge. Murder is *kapu*, but so is walking on the king's land. Women and men must eat separately, and women are not permitted to eat coconuts, bananas, pork or shark meat. The death penalty is applied to all *kapus*.

NANAKOA remembers his older sister, PAUALI. As children, they had played together. They made kites of *kapa* (barkcloth), and PAUALI would thrust the kite high into the air and run down the rocky beach until the trade winds took the kite into the air. They made hand puppets together to act out the stories their mother taught them of how their grandfathers, some 14 generations past, had come to this land from the south, from Bora Bora. The people of old had followed the migrating birds. They brought the coconut and banana palms and sugar cane.

At 14, NANAKOA is almost 6 feet tall. His lanky brown body, stretched on his nine foot wooden surfboard, has

161

tatau (tattoo) marks on its shoulders. These decorative lines on his back had caused him some pain, but his parents and most adults had their bodies and faces covered with the permanent geometric lines and patterns. When PAUALI died, mother had added a *tatau* to her tongue. It was painful, but not as painful as the loss of her only daughter.

From his surfboard, NANAKOA has a fine view of his island home, Hawaii. The waves are not big today, and NANAKOA can see the colorful parrot fish swimming beneath his board in the clear ocean water. Since Hawaii is south of the Tropic of Cancer, it is always warm and usually sunny. The trade winds blow less on the big island than on Maui and Oahu. He could see clouds forming against Mauna Loa; perhaps rain will come later.

Mauna Loa and Mauna Kea, twin volcanos of Hawaii, are truly the tallest mountains on earth if one measures their elevation from the floor of the Pacific Ocean. Even from sea level, Mauna Loa reaches more than 1,300 feet into the clouds. NANAKOA knows that the goddess Pele lives in the volcano; she has been quiet lately. But just ten moons ago, the volcano's explosive eruptions had sent hot lava down the mountainside, through a grove of coconut palms to the shore where the fiery lava met the ocean water with a tremendous hiss of steam.

Umi-a-Liloa, the King of Hawaii, had only ruled nine moons when Pele showed herself at this volcano. The new king decided that Pele was sending him a message to change some of the *kapus*. Now NANAKOA could ride his surfboard and fish at this beach by the king's palace. The old king had kept this place for his personal use by naming it *kapu*. Few dared to risk the punishment of death.

PAUALI had been one who dared. Adventurous and fun loving, she would venture close to the king's land to watch her father dance the hula. Her mother danced, too, but men were the principal dancers. Nanakoa remembered Pauali climbing palm trees with the boys and calling *"Honi kana wikiwiki* (Kiss me quickly)" before she darted away. Pauali knew that bananas were *kapu* for women; she had the body of a woman, but, like a child testing limits, she ate a banana.

Everything happened so quickly that Nanakoa could hardly remember what happened first, the shouts or the stones thrown at his sister. Pauali ran to the water, dove in and began to swim for the City of Refuge. She was a strong swimmer, but the distance was long, past the king's harbor where guards were stationed. Perhaps Pauali should have headed out to deeper water, but she headed straight for safety. A spear from a guard ended her life. Her blood mixed with the warm salt water. Kanaloa, the god of the ocean and the wind, and the god of healing, accepted her spirit and her body. It has been 25 moons, but Nanakoa still misses his sister.

A small *ahi* (yellow finned tuna) appears among the more colorful fish, and the boy spears it. Deftly he secures the wriggling *ahi* in a small net. It is a fine fish, almost as long as his arm. The men paddle their outrigger canoes to deeper waters and catch *ahi* weighing more than a man. Nanakoa, lucky to catch this smaller one, paddles his board quickly toward shore. The net will hold the fish while he catches a wave.

Mother cooks his fish over a fire and serves a generous piece on a *ti* leaf along with taro root cooked in coconut milk. Nanakoa and his father, Kapanoa, eat with the other men.

"You are a fine fisherman, my son." Kapanoa's words of praise are sweeter than sugar cane to Nanakoa.

Some of the men and boys have returned from gathering feathers. Using nets and sticky wands, they have

163

collected feathers without killing the birds. The rare yellow and red feathers are for the robe and helmet the women are making for Umi-a-Liloa. The King's helmet gives him a regal air, but it will take several more years to collect enough yellow feathers to finish the matching cape. They come from the mano bird which is black with a few yellow feathers at his tail. The men may laugh and tease each other about plucking tail feathers from a live bird, but the job is a royal appointment. The men also report that they saw *menehune* (dwarfs) in the hills. They give KAPANOA some more ordinary grey and white feathers to decorate the gourds he uses for dancing.

KAPANOA has a more important job. He is a royal hula dancer. Through dance and words he beseeches the gods to give them success in battle, or good crops or many fish; he is respected for his knowledge and his swaying, expressive hula.

"Father, where do the *menehune* come from?" Nanakoa asks.

"They come out of the ground. They were always here on these islands and once were as numerous as the rats are today," replies KAPANOA. "The old kings defeated them in battle and made them slaves. They are like the *ne ne* (geese), always here. The *menehune* had no dogs or chickens or pigs. They knew of Ku, the god of rain and growth and war, and Kane, the creator of sunlight, but they didn't know how to please the gods."

"Father, I would like to dance among the tiki gods for the King, like you do."

"You? Really?" he replies. "Do you know that you must learn all the stories of our people and the names of all the brave men?"

"I will learn; I will practice and remember."

"Listen to my new chant for our King and remember it," KAPANOA challenges.

When peace and quiet reign
in the government of Hawaii under Umi-a-Liloa,
his name became famous from Hawaii to Kauai.
No king was like him in the administration of government;
he took care of the old men
and the old women and orphans;
he had regard for the people also;
there were no murders and thievings.[31]

NANAKOA has listened intently and adds, "When I learn all the old chants and dances, I want to add a new one. I want to remember my sister, PAUALI."

September

Thursday

After four weeks in the Canary Islands, Cristóbal Colón and his Spanish flotilla are at last ready to sail west. The Niña has new faster sails; the Pinta has a repaired keel; the men have enjoyed fresh food. Their provisions for a year are restocked with fresh water, onions, vegetables, and cheese. They left Palos with a daily ration of one pound biscuit, 2/3 pound of dried meat and fish, and 16 gills[32] of wine for each man.

While the sailors gather wood for cooking aboard ship, Cristóbal goes to the town of Las Palmas and attends mass at the Church of the Ascension. He prays for safety and for the opportunity to tell others of Christ. Colón returns to his flagship and all prepare to weigh anchor. The Santa Maria leads the way, followed by the sister ships, the Niña and the Pinta, captained by the Pinzón brothers. It is more than a month since they left Palos, but their Admiral has made wise decisions already. At 26 degrees north latitude, their sails fill with the trade winds, and they push west and north-west at a fine speed.

1st day of Tishri, 4253, Rosh Hashanah

NATHAN, ESTHER, and their two children have only been in Amsterdam for a month. In Cadiz, Spain, Jews were required to wear a special hat and a patch on their clothing. Here, they have more freedom. It is a port like their former home, Cadiz, but it is actually a city below sea level. The small house they have rented is on wooden pilings in the mushy ground. Amsterdam began more than 200 years ago when people built a dam on the Amstel River, and dikes on the Zuider Zee. They dug canals and used the dredgings to build up the land. The Zuider Zee forms a large natural harbor from the North Sea, and Amsterdam is a busy port for trading in northern Europe.

The Spanish family has been trying to get used to wooden shoes, herring, Gouda cheese, and the Dutch language. So much is new, that they are happy to find other Jewish families to join with in celebrating the High Holy Days. Rosh Hashanah means "beginning year", and this one is an especially new beginning. ESTHER bakes the traditional holiday bread and puts a little dove made of dough on it to symbolize prayers going up to God. In Amsterdam, they learn to dip slices of apple, as well as the bread, into honey, and eat them with the old blessing, "May it be a sweet and good year."

The Jewish year is 4,253 since God created the heavens and the earth. Going to the synagogue reminds the Spanish Jews of home. The cantor blows the shofar ram's horn, and the Rabbi prays, "Our Father, Our King, we have sinned before you." Only at this time of year do Jews lie prostrate on the floor. They confess their misdeeds

168

and promise to do better in the next year. In order to receive forgiveness, everyone needs to forgive others. For NATHAN, it is especially hard to forgive someone who has taken his home and disrupted his work and family.

The Rabbi reminds all, "When Joseph's brothers sold him into slavery in Egypt, it was an evil deed, but God used it for good. When famine struck Israel, they were able to go to Egypt and get grain from Joseph and Pharaoh."

NATHAN thinks, "Amsterdam is a busier port than Cadiz. And the nearby Rhine River leads to more great trading cities. I can learn Dutch, and deal in gilders, and make loans and purchases. God can use evil for good."

The Rabbi continues, "If you are wicked and do not change, if you do not forgive, God will write your name in the book of the dead."

ESTHER is in the back with the women. "It has been so unfair," she thinks. "I can learn to cook pea soup and herring, but I wonder if smoked eel is even Kosher; I'm sure that the Zeeland oysters aren't!"

They have come to the Netherlands, the low countries. When God created the earth 4,253 years ago, He knew this land under the sea could be redeemed for them to live and walk on. Each Jew has ten days to get right with God and his fellow man for the new year.

As they leave the synagogue and cross a canal, NATHAN stops on the bridge, takes Esther's hand and says to her, "May you be written in the book of life for a good year!" It is a traditional Rosh Hashanah greeting, but it has never had more meaning for them.

Saturday

Pinturicchio has been employed by Pope Alexander VI to decorate the Hall of Saints in his Vatican apartments. When the artist did the frescoes for Pope Sixtus ten years ago, he assisted Perugino and gained his nickname "pinturicchio", meaning second-rate painter, and he is called this by the Borgias, rather than Bernardino di Betto, his Christian name. Lucretia, 12, and her brother, Cesare, 16, are posing for the artist as central characters. Cesare is Emperor Maximinus, and Lucretia, St. Catherine of Alexandria, who is disputing with him. She is counting on her fingers the reasons for her Christian faith. Pinturicchio has sketched a lavish scene for the 26 foot long fresco. In the center is a triumphal arch topped with the Borgia bull. Trees and birds fill the sky, and men, women, children and dogs crowd around the delicate Catherine and the Egyptian King Maximinus on his canopied throne. This St. Catherine is the patron of bastards. Not only does Pope Alexander openly acknowledge his children, but also his mistress who lives in the Borgia apartments.

Pope Alexander enters, "How are you, my children?" he inquires of Cesare and Lucretia. "How goes the decorating?" he addresses Pinturicchio.

"Fine." "Fine."

Alexander's authority is obvious. After thirty-five years as vice-chancellor, head of the Curia, he is a Pope of action and power. There were more than 200 murders in Rome in the month between Innocent's death and Roderigo Borgia's election as Pope. The lawlessness of Rome is abating under his swift, stern justice. Alexander has made a public example by hanging a murderer and his brother and burning their house. He is also swift in recalling painters to decorate his apartments.

His secretary enters the Hall of Saints. "Your Holiness," he bows, "please excuse the interruption, but the Great Turk has been asking to see you."

"Send him in; we will see him now."

Djem, popularly referred to as the Great Turk, is the brother of the Ottoman Sultan. He is the hostage of the Pope, but he is not in fetters. He is confined, but in pleasant surroundings. Djem has maintained his dignity through a ten year imprisonment. The large white turban he wears gives him an exotic appearance.

"Great Pope," Djem begins, "you have the spear that pierced the side of Jesus, a gift from my brother, Bayazid. I can help you get more holy relics; you can have the land where your Jesus was born and taught. Let me lead your army to Jerusalem." Djem has prepared this speech for the new Pope.

Alexander laughs, not just heartily, but derisively. "No!" he bellows, "No!" This simpleton believes Alexander's boasts of warring against the Turks in the Holy Land. The Christian rulers of Europe may talk of another crusade, but they are more interested in getting territory from each other, as Alexander understands. He gives no further attention to his prisoner, but turns to his artist.

"Pinturicchio, how goes my Hall of Saints?"

"The Saint Catherine sketches are here. I am almost ready to begin the fresco," the artist responds.

"I like the arch in the center; it will be strong in that arched space." The Pope continues, "Don't hesitate to use many gold accents. We can always get more gold." He glances at his valuable hostage.

171

"I wonder if I might pose Djem in the crowd?" Pinturicchio inquires. "He would lend a feeling of Egypt to the scene."

"Certainly. He might as well be useful to someone!" Alexander agrees. "Since Turks are in short supply in Rome, use him twice."

Tuesday

The three ships of Cristóbal Colón had been sailing 50 to 54 leagues[33] a day. The square sails caught the trade winds and sped them west and north from 26 degrees north latitude to 30 degrees north latitude. One week ago, Colón had dropped his longest chain to 200 fathoms[34] and did not touch bottom. Then the winds abated.

The doldrums test the patience of every sailor. Sometimes, the air is perfectly still for hours or even days, and when winds come, they are weak and fluctuating. Cristóbal sits in his cabin and records in the official log that they have sailed 13 leagues today. He believes he has gone 21 leagues and records that in his private journal which he is careful to hide from the men.

Cristóbal knows his direction by the compass; he estimates his speed. After calculating the distance traveled each day, he logs a lesser amount in the official log for the benefit of his impatient men. Surprisingly, this is the more accurate figure as Colón tends to overestimate the speed of his little flotilla.

A shout goes up from the Pinta, *"Tierra*! Land!"* Martin Pinzón, the captain, has seen land. Some think they could see it too, but most are doubtful.

Juan de la Cosa, the pilot of the Santa Maria jokes, "We are in so much sea weed that it looks like land right under our bow. It looks like the sargasso grapes that the Portuguese grow!"

Juan had owned the Santa Maria when she was the Mary Gallant. He is proud to be on the biggest ship. Its central deck between the forecastle and the aftcastle is

173

longer than the entire Niña or Pinta, more than 60 feet. Big or small, in the Sargasso Sea no one moves very quickly.

10th day of Tishri, 4253

The great city of Jerusalem is desolate and in ruins, but is still home to 4,000 families. The Dome of the Rock built in the first rush of Islam in 691 C.E. stands, walls and golden dome, but has been damaged by fire. The Mameluke rulers are Islamic but are more involved in Cairo. They have been zealous in driving the Christians away, so the Church of the Holy Sepulcher and other Christian sites are also in disrepair. The Jewish population is accepted; after all, they haven't launched crusades. Seventy-five Jewish families live in Jerusalem. Three families from Barcelona and two from Zaragosa are recent arrivals.

Yom Kippur is a serious time for the individual Jew and the community. The families from Zaragosa are related, and their hearts are heavy because they have left an old grandmother and two young adults behind. Those from Barcelona are still stunned by the cruelty of the sea captains. During the nights at sea, Jews would disappear and the next day sailors appeared wearing their rings. All are surprised how little remains of the Great Temple in Jerusalem; the Dome of the Rock stands where Solomon's temple once stood. They gather in a synagogue. Everyone removes his shoes as he enters to signify that they are on holy ground. This is the time to forgive and accept one another, to *kippur* (get rid of) quarrels and start a new year together.

Rabbi Obadiah Bertinoro is sensitive to the newest members of his congregation. "God will forgive all who repent, even those who denied him and were baptized as

175

Christians, because they were forced, can return to the one Almighty Creator, our Lord."

The fasting began at sundown last night. Their Islamic neighbors know the Jews will fast all night and day. Moslems fast too and understand getting right with God, but Moslems don't fully appreciate the responsibility Jews feel to the entire community. During the High Holy Days from Rosh Hashanah to Yom Kippur, debts are forgiven, atonement is made, and a new year begins with promises to do better individually and for the whole community.

In the synagogue, the white curtains that cover the ark are parted and the cantor removes the Torah scrolls. He chants the "Kol Nidrei," the all vows prayer. The High Holy Days of the new year have come to this last chance to be right with God. All vows are forgiven. When little JOSHUA was so sick on the boat from Barcelona, his father JONATHAN promised God he would give all he had to the poor if JOSHUA would live. JOSHUA is fine, but JONATHAN's family would suffer if he gave away what little he has been able to bring from Spain. He must truly forgive those Spaniards who harmed him, and God will forgive and release him from his vow. Moslems and Christians sometimes interpret this to mean that a Jew can renege on a promise or contract, but this forgiveness applies only to vows with God.

The cantor continues to sing the Kol Nidrei.

Our vows shall not be vows; our oaths shall not be oaths.

When the shofar is blown at sundown, the fast ends and the new year really begins. God created the heavens and the earth 4,253 years ago. It is up to Obadiah and JONATHAN and Jews in Jerusalem and everywhere to make the world a better place in the new year, so the Messiah will come and rule.

Jerosolima nomē vrbis in palestina metropolis iudeoꝛ:pꝛi⁹ Jeb⁹.postea salē. tercio bierosolima. vltio bella dicta.Cuius vrbis pꝛim⁹ ꝑditoꝛ fuit(vt Joseph⁹ testaꝰ) Canaan q̃ suꝰ appellaꝰ erat rex. Et b q̃dē mel chiledech sacerdos dei altissimi dicebatur. Qui cū ibidē pbanū edificassꝛ illud Solimā appellauit.solimi fuerūt ppli iuxta liciā q̃s bomer⁹ puꝑ gnatissimos:ꝛ a belleropbōte deuictos dicit. et in mōub⁹bitasse.Et cornelis⁹ tacit⁹cū de iudeoꝛ oꝛigine opiōe narrat ait.Alij clara iudeoꝛ initia solimos carmib⁹ celebꝛatā bomeri gētē ꝝdi tam vꝛbē bierosolimā noie suo fecisse. vñ Juuenalis interpꝛes legū solimaꝛ. q̃ ciuitas cananee gētis vsꝗ ad tpa dauid regi bitatio fuit. ꝏec io sue iudeoꝛū pꝛiceps eos cananeos seu iebusfeos expellere potuit.Dauid iebusseis expulsis cū aꝰ nitatem reedificasset eā bierosolimā.i.munitissiꝭmā nūcupauit.Dns⁹ vꝛb situs ꝛ munitio petroꝰ sa erat.ꝛ triplici muro cingebatur.q̃ vt Strabo sit inten⁹ adps abundans exteri⁹ vo oino siccam fossam bēbat i lapide excisam.xl.pedū ꝑfundiꝰ tate.latitudo vo.cc.l.E lapide aūt exciso educta erant celeberrimi tēpli menia.ꝏec bierosolima lōge clarissima vrbium oꝛiētis suꝑ duos colles erat ꝝdita iteruallo discretos i quā dom⁹creberꝛ rime desinebāt.Collū alter q̃ supioꝛ citas excelsioꝛ ꝛ i.pliꝛitate directioꝛ castellu dauid dicebaꝰ tur.Alter q̃ iserioꝛ sustinet citates vndiꝗ decliꝭ nis e vall⁹ i medio ad syloā ptins ita fōte q̃ dulcē e vocabāt.firmissime āt do salomois alioꝛūꝗ i

terra regū opa oꝛnata fuit.agrippa eē ptez citatꝰ addiderat ꝛ cinxerat.Eruberas eī nisitudine paulati extra menia ꝑbebat.ꝏoiata ē pꝭ addiꝭ ta noua citas.Qñe āt citatꝰ i giro spaciū.xxx.ꝰ trib⁹ stadijs finiebaꝰ.Et si i toto admirabiꝰ.ter cius mur⁹ admirabilioꝛ ob excellētias turrꝝ q̃ ad septētrioné occidētēꝗ surgebat i ꝝgulo.de q̃ soꝰ le oꝛto arabia .pspici poterat ꝛ mare vsꝗ ad fiꝭ nes bebꝛeoꝛ.Et iuxta eā turrꝝ yppico:ꝛ due q̃s berodes i ātꝗ muro edificauerat.Mirabilꝰ fuit lapidū magnitudo ex secto marmoꝛe cādido ita adduati vt singlte turres singlta saxa videreꝰ .bijs i septētriōalj pte aula ꝝgia pstātissima .ꝛiūgebaꝰ tur.Muro alto cincta acꝛvarietate saxoꝛū oꝛnata Alte dencꝗ pꝛtic⁹ ꝑ arclim flere colūneꝗ i sinꝭ gulis:q̃ iter eas sb diuo patebāt spacia vbi erāt viridaria ai alternis eneis.qb⁹ aꝗ effundebaꝰ. Pudet dicere b ꝝgia q̃l⁹fuerat cū flāma ab itestiꝭ nis isidiatoꝛib⁹ oia .psumpsit.De excidio trꝰ b⁹ regie vꝛb isen⁹ patebit:vꝛbē aūt sacras reddidit moꝛs xpi.Plaqꝗ saꝰ i eo loco videre possumus Amne.s.q̃ lotꝰ e xps.Tēplū seu tēplꝰ ruinas i q̃ wcuit.locivbt cū sūma būilitate passus e coꝛpe vt nos ai passionib⁹ libaret.sepulcꝛ vbi sacinssiꝭ mū illo coꝛp⁹ bstitit.Et vñ ascēdit in celū. q̃ ad iudiciū fuersū⁹ credit .vbi vēꝭ⁊ fluenb⁹ipauit vbi reicꝗ elegit idoctos atꝗ iopes piscatoꝛes.q̃ꝭ rū bamis ꝛ rbetib⁹piscareꝰ ipatoꝛes ꝛ ꝝges gēꝭ tius.vbi cecos illūiauit.lepꝛofos mūdauit.paꝰ raliticos erexit.moꝛtuos suscitauit.Multaqꝗ ꝛ alia q̃ lōge pseꝗ tedioꝛi eēt.cū ex euāge.nō sint

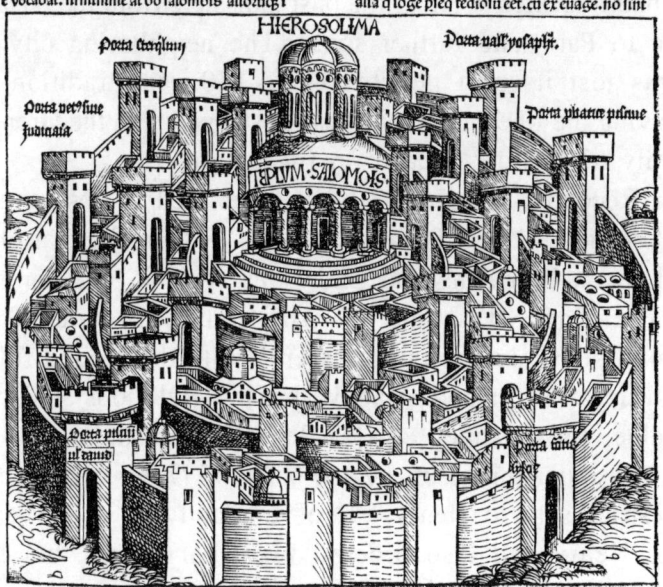

Jerusalem and King Soloman's Temple. A European view from Hartman Schedel's *Liber Chronicarum*. Nuremberg: 1493, Anton Koberger. Reproduced by courtesy of The Pierpont Morgan Library, New York. PML 180, folio XVII. Woodcut by Michael Wohlgemut, page from the *World Chronicle* of Nuremberg. Refer to October 25, page 190.

Saturday

The art of tapestry flourishes in the Old World and the New. In the city of Tournai, Pasquier Grenier has guided his family business into a major industry for his city. He insists on the finest wool yarns, subtle in hue and texture, and precious gold and silver threads for luster and elegance. He sees that the snippets of thread of precious metals are saved for recycling, but he is not miserly, just practical. He is enjoying the success of his hard work, intelligence, and a bit of luck. Just thirteen years ago, Louis XI had relocated some of the best tapissiers from the Alsace area to Paris and further south. The neighboring city of Arras lost its best people. Their 150 year tradition of weaving the finest tapestries was destroyed, and the Grenier family of Tournai is eager to fill this spot.

Recently, Charles VIII has attempted to restore the craftsmen to Arras. Pasquier Grenier is thankful that God had given him sons and grandsons with an eye for the weavers art. It seems to him that more and more commissions are for hunting scenes with the ground filled with tiny flowers and meadow grasses. Religious subjects, whether for an abbey or a castle, seem less in demand.

Pasquier thinks of *The History of Troy*, eleven huge tapestries sent to Henry VII of England just three years ago. Henry had also ordered two altar pieces, but the delight for the tapissier was in creating those exotic scenes crowded with heroes, horses, tents, lances, and the beautiful Helen of Troy. The Greniers' export license provides more opportunities for the future of John and Antoine. He tells his sons, "When I was a young tapissier, we would make

178

five scenes of Esther and Ahasuerus or of our Lord Jesus for every one of history. Now people want 'The Knight of China'."

The elder Pasquier no longer takes the bobbins of fine wool into his hands. His master craftsmen, journeymen and apprentices sit behind the taut warp of flax strung on a frame. Looking in a mirror to check their progress, they also constantly refer to the cartoon, a full scale rendition on paper, not only for the pattern but for color specifications. Each man has a portion of the cartoon, and shoulder to shoulder they sit before the loom, passing the shuttles to the right and left.

The Greniers believe in giving the customer what he wants, and even the abbeys want hunting scenes! But he wonders how his grandson has visualized the wild-men and women with strange beasts in his newest design. Perhaps he has heard stories of the sailors from Lisbon, of dark skinned people west of Iceland, or their stories and ivory carvings from the realm of the Mani Kongo in Africa excited the imagination. Rather than reliving the past, these new designs seem to anticipate future adventures.

Half way around our globe in Cuzco, llama wool is on the bobbins. The technique is the same; this wool waft thread is carefully placed between the sturdy warp, covering it completely. With a comb, the wool is tamped to a tight and precise position. In Cuzco, orangy-red and black are popular colors. Patterns there have been used for more than 1000 years. Monkeys in trees and stylized cats are fashionable today. These patterns give some continuity to a series of cultures in the Andes mountains where written language has not developed.

The Incas excel in architecture, roads, gold work, weaving and tapestry. For weaving, the warp is visible and

179

becomes part of the pattern, but in a true tapestry it is completely covered.

The Inca robes and blankets are woven by the hundreds of virgins from good families who live in a large compound next to the temple of the Sun. Some use large free-standing looms, similar to those in Tournai, but most girls use the popular back-strap loom. The weaver provides the tension on the warp by tying those threads to a tree or peg and leaning back on the frame behind her hips. She might stand or sit, but the width of the fabric is limited to the span of her arms. Should she be noticed by the Inca, a girl will move into the royal household. Blankets provide the main furnishings, not only for sleeping, but stacked for sitting. Sleeveless tunics, worn by men and women are sometimes woven of cotton. Finer garments use vicuna hair, alpaca, or even bird feathers. Golden threads are not a part of Inca weavings or tapestry, perhaps because it is not as precious as in Europe.

Great sheets of gold decorate the temple of the Sun. Gold and silver ornaments of animals and plants vie with nature for beauty in gardens. The virgin weavers are fed on dishes of silver and gold. These luxurious objects did not excuse the able-bodied from work. Indeed, laziness is a crime, punishable by death. Even the great Sun God endorses work. The Inca name for gold is "the sweat of the sun".

October

Friday

The commander of the Santa Maria carefully logs the distance traveled by his flagship and the two caravels. It is a month since they have left the Canary Islands. He woke this morning thinking he was Cristoforo Colombo of Genoa: a weaver's son, a pious adventurer and idealist, a visionary. But quickly he became Cristóbal Colón: a Spaniard, a maker of charts and maps, a sailor since the age of fourteen. He must control his rebellious sailors. Some are beginning to demand the ships turn back. He must be convincing and firm with his men before he can hope to gain the title of "Great Admiral of the Ocean" and become governor of the lands that lay west. If his brother had secured financing from Henry VII of England, he would be answering to "Christopher Columbus". That name had a newness that pleases him in this new situation.

Closing his log books, Christopher leaves the official one on his desk and secrets the other behind his treasured manuscript of Marco Polo's travels. If only Polo's book were printed, more people would be interested in finding a way to Cathay. The cabin boy will ignore Marco Polo, but he might check the log.

Brilliant sunlight and warm moist air greet the commander as he leaves his dark cabin. As the men notice his arrival on deck, some of the grumbling subsides. As of today, Friday, October 5, the Niña, the Pinta, and the Santa Maria have sailed almost 2000 miles, averaging 72 miles a day.

In 1484, in his proposal to John II of Portugal, Columbus had estimated finding land after sailing west

2400 miles. The learned men of the Portuguese court found this a ridiculously low estimate. It was low for reaching China by sailing west, but it was quite accurate for reaching the New World. Even eight years ago, most learned men had agreed that the world is round and that sailing west could bring one to Cathay.

Christopher scans the horizon with his spy glass, the complete circle. He descends the ladder from the aftcastle to the main deck and walks purposefully to the forecastle. He thinks of telling the men about the pearls and gold Marco Polo had found, but they have heard it before. Two seated sailors look at him defiantly, jaws and bodies set, and he is obliged to walk around them.

Looking west from the bow, Columbus sees two specks. Wiping his spy glass, he looks again and sees three, maybe four, birds.

"Diego" he orders one of the sullen sailors, "Come here."

Diego moves slowly.

"Hurry, if you want to see the birds through my glass!"

The news spreads quickly through the crew. Fernando and Isabella had offered a prize of 10,000 maravedis to the first man to sight land. When, after a month at sea, birds are sighted, the watch for land intensifies. All eyes face west.

Friday

Florence would like to claim Piero della Francesca as her son, but he belongs to the mountains to the east, Umbria. Today, Piero died in Borgo San Sepolco, where he was born 72 years ago. Here, his mortal remains rest near his fresco masterpiece of the Resurrection. A triumphal Christ dominates the center of the composition, stepping out of the tomb. Piero used himself as a model for one of the soldiers stunned by this miracle. The landscape background reflects the great transformation that has occurred, dead trees to the left, healthy, leafy trees to the right.

Just over the crest of the Appenines, Piero had done portraits of the great Federigo Montefeltro, Duke of Urbino, and his wife Batista. Federigo had called Piero to Urbino twenty years ago as Batista was dying, so he might have an image of his beloved wife. Federigo joined her in ten years, but their son, Guidobaldo continues his father's patronage of the arts.

The Ducal palace, its high brick walls covered with gleaming marble, is a fortress in the Umbrian hills but also a center for learning and the arts. Federigo's books are housed in a library superbly crafted of inlaid woods designed to trick the eye to see open cupboards and pet birds, where flat doors are the reality. Guidobaldo supports Giovanni Santi, a painter and poet who lives just two-hundred yards from the palace. Giovanni's eight-year-old son, Raphael, often accompanies him to the palace.

184

When Raphael was born, Giovanni insisted that his wife nurse their baby, although they could afford a wet nurse, which was the norm for people of their station. The father continued to lavish attention upon his son, teaching him to be thoughtful and courteous. Now father and son have been drawn closer together by death. First the boy's older brother and sister died and then his beloved mother. Grieving Giovanni, bearing full responsibility for his young son, has been teaching Raphael to draw and paint.

Together, at the Ducal Palace, Giovanni and Raphael Santi study the paintings of Paulo Uccello and Piero della Francesca's fine portraits of the late Duke and Duchess. When the child has absorbed the beauty of the two profile portraits, the father comments, "Do you see that Duke Federigo had a broken nose and heavy jowls? Yet his portrait is as beautiful as the lovely Batista." Giovanni instructs with a question, "What is Piero's secret?"

Raphael looks but cannot decide.

"Give me your hand," his father gently guides the child's hand to trace in the air the profile of the Duke. "It is the line!"

"It is the line," Raphael repeats, but he truly understands.

"Look closely a few more minutes, and then I will have a surprise for you," a fatherly pat on the shoulder accompanies the directive.

While the child studies Batista, Giovanni removes the other portrait from the wall. "Look, here's a picture on the back. Isn't that a surprise? A two-sided painting."

Piero della Francesca's landscape of the Umbrian hills is another treat for the eyes of Raphael.

Friday

It's 2:00 A.M. on a moonlit night in the West Indies. From the crow's nest of the Pinta comes a cry, "Land! *Tierra!*" Rodrigo de Triana's voice has such authority that Captain Martin Pinzón appears from his cabin. He has continued to be negative after the land he sighted 2 1/2 weeks ago disappeared in the morning light. In the week since Columbus saw birds, the faster Niña has been the first to spot more birds, including land birds, and branches floating in the water. But when the weary Martin climbs the mast to the crow's nest, he is positive he sees land. He directs his brother Francisco, the pilot, to watch for reefs, and he personally fires the signal gun.

The Santa Maria and the Niña respond, and soon all decks are filled with men. The moon has been up three hours. As the land draws closer, the men on all the ships sing hymns and pray, thanking God. When the sun rises at their backs, they see that the land appears to be an island.

Christopher Columbus dresses to meet the Emperor of Cipangu, Japan. They have been at sea 37 days since the Canary Islands; it is 71 days since they left Palos. The ships drop anchor in a natural harbor.

Small skiffs are lowered into the water and rowed to the shore where some of the younger members of the Taino tribe have gathered to observe the three large ships. They watch the pale strangers come ashore. Are these white men gods? Sons of heaven? The strangers kneel on the ground briefly; they have feathers which they dip into a black liquid and make marks on a sort of large pale leaf.

Columbus has officially recorded the landing. He plants a flag of Spain and the cross of the Catholic Church and announces, "I claim this land for God and for the King and Queen of Spain."

The Tainos seem innocent children of God. They wear little clothing. Their hair is black and coarse like the tail of a horse, with bangs to their eyebrows, and worn long in back. Luis de Torres's attempts at translation are not as effective as gestures and the offering of gifts of mirrors and beads. Christopher tries to ask directions to the Emperor of Japan. Martin Pinzón asks about gold.

The Tainos wonder at the clothing on these white skinned people. Three brave young Indians venture closer to touch the shirts and doublets and the white skin beneath them. The long hair on the strangers is much like their own, but some of them have hair on their faces. The white skin under the shirts does not seem to match the colorful legs, encased in stockings. The Indians observe that several men have tails. The three braves grab hold of the "tails" and are surprised and pained to find their hands bleeding from their first encounter with Spanish swords.

Sunday

Columbus records in his journal, "The first island I discovered, I gave the name San Salvador, in honor of His Divine Majesty, who has wondrously granted all this. The Indians call it Guanahani." [36]

Appearing on deck, he directs the pilot, Juan de la Cosa, "Set sail for the south. That is the way to Cathay and Kublai Khan."

They have taken seven Indian men on board the Santa Maria. They might help with translation when they meet other Indians or provide more directions. Certainly they will amaze the Spanish.

Their fellow Tainos watch from shore:

"These men are not gods. They are no better than the fierce Caniba who steal our children."

"They may find gold in Cuba-nacan."

"They certainly were excited about finding gold."

"I'm glad they are leaving Guanahani."

Luis and Christopher heard 'Cathay' when 'Caniba' was spoken. They hear 'Kublai Khan' when the Indians pointed towards 'Cuba-nacan'. Sailing south, they are missing a chance to land on the North American mainland, a few miles to the west.

Tuesday

Alexander VII covets the power and glory of Alexander the Great. Few dare to refute or refuse a Pope, particularly a Borgia Pope. Alexander has dissolved his daughter Lucretia's marriage contract in Spain and has betrothed her to Giovanni Sforza, Lord of Pisaro. For his son, Jofre, Alexander is negotiating for the daughter of Alfonso II, Prince of Naples. Should Charles of France press his claim to Naples, Alfonso might appreciate a Papal alliance.

On official business, the Pope has summoned Bramante to Rome. This architect was born Donato d'Agnolo near Urbino, but was nicknamed Bramante because of his intense personality. A painter at first, Bramante's interest in perspective soon led him into more architectural and sculptural commissions. Twenty years ago the Sforzas had summoned him to Milan to complete the great cathedral. His designs for the cathedral there have not been executed, but his church of Santa Maria and the Great Hospital courtyard have brought him fame. His Cathedral at Lake Como shows his skills in combining the classical orders and domes of ancient Rome into glorious buildings. In Milan, Bramante outshines Leonardo, and Alexander wants him in Rome.

The Pope will wait to appoint a new bishop of Beijing. Alexander needs money, and why should he pay the Bishop who has no chance of arriving at his diocese? Officially, twenty-four year old Alexander Farnese is appointed Cardinal.[37] Unofficially, the new cardinal's sister should show her appreciation, for she is the Pope's mistress.

189

Thursday

Half way between Venice and Antwerp, Nuremberg, in the foothills of the Bohemian forest, sees itself as the center of the world. Its 20,000 inhabitants are governed by an elected council, but only forty-three families vote and pass the responsibilities of government among their numbers. All 75 to 100 million inhabitants of Europe may not know of Nuremberg, but Nurembergers have a view of the world.

Martin Behaim has completed the first terrestrial globe. Somehow the human mind had conceived of the heavens as a sphere and depicted the stars, zodiac and constellations on a giant ball, but Martin was the first to give a physical representation to the global earth being discussed in universities and courts from Krakow to Lisbon. Europe is enlarged compared to Asia and Africa. West of Greenland and Iceland, Behaim shows a great ocean stretching over half the globe to Japan.

Hartmann Scheldel is completing his *World Chronicle*. Beginning with the creation of the world, it continues to the present giving histories of important cities including Rome, Bologna, Lyon, and Argentina, a silver mining city on the Rhine. Scheldel has completed his text in Latin and is preparing a German version. Scholars everywhere read Latin, but more and more German readers are buying books. The schools of Nuremberg are continually increasing literacy in town; Nuremberg has the first upper school in Germany for students ages 12 to 17.

Writing the history of the world, Scheldel's part, is just the beginning of producing the *World Chronicle*, a large book of 335 leaves weighing fourteen pounds. The paper is a major expense, but Nuremberg is a leader in paper making using manufacturing skills to produce a uniform thickness and color. The moveable type is also made here; each letter is cast from an alloy of lead, tin and antimony giving the type resistance to wear, but a soft surface to hold the ink. Typemakers stay in business not only with replacements, but to outfit new printing shops in Nuremberg.

The biggest shop belongs to Anton Koberger, the leading printer in all of Europe. He owns fifteen presses and employs 70 men at his printshop and bindery. He produces five or six titles a year. The *World Chronicle* is his most ambitious to date. It is designed to complement the Gutenberg Bible, but without the hand painted additions to the typeset pages, except by special order.

Michael Wolgemuth has been working on the illustrations for four years. He had no trouble drawing scenes of Noah's Ark and King Solomon's Temple. Even his apprentice, Albrecht Dürer had contributed a scene of three skeletons dancing, while Death plays a tune, and another woodcut showing Ulysses on his boat while Circe attempts to lure him and his Greek warriors onto her island. To illustrate current history, Wolgemuth has traveled to Augsberg, Mainz, Munich, Vienna, Magdeburg, and Strasbourg. He sketches each city in its distinct location showing steeples, bridges and landmarks. Then, he carefully draws the city on a block of wood. Assistants carve away the unmarked wood, and with a few final touches, the block is ready to receive the ink. Koberger must lay out the woodcuts and the type settings to fill each page in a beautiful and logical way. Combining woodcuts and moveable type has been accepted for thirty years. The competition between the two forms of printing vanished almost as quickly as it began.

The fifty-eight year old Wolgemuth is a superb craftsman. His title page of God creating the cosmos was completed and printed in 1490. He is paid by Seybald Schreyer and Sebastian Cammermaister, who are financing the entire project. Wolgemuth's step-son has been assisting him since young Dürer left.

Anton Koberger is a fine organizer. Wolgemuth has done 28 portraits of Popes, and Koberger reuses them over and over for the most important of the 226 Popes. Woodcuts of 44 crowned heads represent 270 kings. The artist's scene of Mainz serves to illustrate Naples, Aquileia, Bologna, and Lyon.

The *Saxon Chronicle* has just been published in Mainz. Scheldel's Nuremberg chronicles, nearing completion, will be bigger and better. He makes no mention of the Portuguese sailing around Africa or the Spanish sailing west. Nuremberg has a 500 year history. Its sons, like Veit Stoss in Krakow, the older Albrecht Dürer in the court of Frederick III, and the younger Albrecht Dürer, journeyman artist in Basel, make their mark in the world but call Nuremberg home. Anton Koberger can stay here and influence the world with his books. His recent wedding to Margaret Holtschuker has brought him much happiness. His first wife, Ursula, died after the birth of their eighth child. Although his friends and neighbors, like the Dürers, were a help, it is good to have a wife again.[38] It is good to live between Venice and Antwerp in the center of the world.

Saturday

From the deck of the Great Harry, Henry VII commands the siege of Boulogne. His new ship is a visible sign that the English Navy is a force of considerable and growing power. Smaller vessels have delivered Henry's army across the English Channel to the coast of Brittany, and foot soldiers have blocked land access to Boulogne as effectively as Henry's ships control the seas.

Much of Brittany had been lost by Henry VI, a king more revered for his saintly qualities and love of education than his military prowess. The young heiress of Brittany, Anne, married Charles, King of France, less than a year ago, and Charles is determined to keep the English on their side of the channel.

Dear little Anne needed a defender. Almost two years ago, when she was fourteen, she was married by proxy to Maximillian, King of the Romans, a 41 year old widower. Anne got into bed nude, and Maximillian's proxy sat on the bed and took his feet off the floor to legally consummate the marriage. Maximillian continued to be preoccupied with battles and politics and never met Anne. Charles came to her rescue last November.

Although the twenty-one year old Charles seemed ugly to some, hunch-backed, with wide hoof-like feet, he was literally a knight in shining armor to Anne. He was skillful in jousts and battle, but in negotiations he was unexcelled. Henry's army was then conducting a siege at Rennes, and hadn't been paid in months. Charles paid them to leave. Then he contacted Pope Innocent to annul Anne's marriage to Maximillian, and within a month they were married.

Anne, at fifteen, learned that there was more to consummating a marriage than feet off the floor. She had a protector and a lover, and Charles had Brittany.

Henry's persistence is a nuisance, a naval exercise. Boulogne has supplies to withstand a two-year siege. Charles isn't interested in attacking England; his eyes are on Naples. It is time to negotiate again.

"Permission to come aboard?" The request comes from the skiff which has come alongside the Great Harry.

"Granted." Henry's captains have come from Boulogne with news.

"Your Highness, Charles is offering to settle old debts so that we may live in peace. He is offering 500,000 gold crowns owed from the Treaty of Picquagny if you will withdraw your siege of Boulogne."[39]

"That is interesting." Henry replies, "He offers to settle a debt contracted when he was a puking baby. I'll wager he'll give more! How goes the siege?"

"Boulogne has water and provisions," the captain replies, "and they have shelter. With another cold winter beginning, our soldiers will suffer more than Boulogne."

"I need more gold; my expenses in Brittany have been large." For Henry, financial considerations are paramount. "And I want Charles to deal with that imposter, Perkin Warbeck.[40] Then I will consider lifting the siege."

"Yes, Your Highness."

"Go and tell the French King my conditions."

November

Thursday' All Saints Day

On the banks of the Guadalquiver River is the Triana district of Sevilla. The dockyards there abound in sailors, shipwrights, sailmakers, merchants, and young boys poorly fed and never paid, who serve as apprentices. One of their shore duties is to catch a healthy cat, for every ship needs an agile mouser to keep the stow-away rats and mice in check.

Amerigo Vespucci loves to visit this dock area. The 41 year old seaman is employed as the Medici agent in Sevilla. He deals in letters of credit, gold florins, and loans for trading ventures. Within this year he has been in Barcelona, Florence and Cadiz. He is equally at home in the dock yard or across the Guadalquiver in central Sevilla.

Only the Giralda tower remains of the mosque of Islam that once dominated Sevilla. The city fathers have almost incorporated the tower into their enormous Gothic cathedral. They have succeeded in building the largest cathedral in the world. It is not just soaring or vast, but elephantine. Ornately carved wooden altars strive valiantly to fill the cavernous interior. Although the cathedral has replaced the mosque, the Alcazar and its garden remain. Moslem craftsmen skilled in colorful tile, graceful arches and inviting patios, have continued to work for Christian employers. This Mudejar fashion adds one more level of style and considerable charm to the buildings of Sevilla.

As a Medici representative, Amerigo Vespucci has a handsome wooden chest for his papers. Its Plateresque style imitates silver sculpting in its ornate detail carved into furniture and room panels. The Medicis would appreciate the gift of a plateresque sideboard. It might be more sensible to ship a carver to Florence than to export these massive chests. Florence buys sword blades from Toledo, and sells sail cloth and rope to Sevilla. Gianetto Berardi even shipped Spanish horses to Florence. Amerigo had been instructed to avoid speculative entanglements.

Amerigo has heard of the small enterprise of the Indies led by Cristóbal Colón, of Genoa. Since Bartholomeo Dias completed the journey around Africa five years ago, China seems nearer by sailing East. Amerigo wonders what Cristóbal and his small flotilla will find sailing West.

Saturday

Êtaples is just ten miles south of the sieged town of Boulogne. Henry VII, in full armor, is here to sign the official treaty ending the siege with the representatives of Charles VIII. The French King has agreed to pay 745,000 gold crowns and to give no aid or assistance to Perkin Warbeck, alias the Duke of York. This upstart Fleming commoner claims to be Richard, the younger son of Edward IV; he is so convincing that people follow him, and this is a threat to the Tudor monarchy.

England agrees to withdraw from Boulogne, and to refrain from alliances with Maximillian. Henry is relieved to be free of that entanglement. Henry, fluent in French, English and Latin, signs with a flourish and departs north to command the end of the siege and await news of Charles' signature and the payment of the gold.

Sunday

As the three caravels draw close to shore, Indians in canoes and even some hardy swimmers come to meet them. Although the explorers have sailed to a new bay, they are still on the island they had named Fernando when they arrived seventeen days ago. The news has spread overland to the Arawaks about the gifts the white men bring; so the Indians have come to welcome them and satisfy their own curiosity.

Luis de Torres has had some success in communicating. The Arawak language is a challenge to a man who knows Chaldean, Arabic and Hebrew. The Arawaks welcome them to their village of 3,000 people where some are nobles, some commoners, and some slaves. Each of the 1,000 homes has a statue representing a *zemis* spirit which the family reveres. They have farm lands outside their village. The Spanish are happy to trade some beads for a pepper pot stew of meat, vegetables and peppers cooked in manioc juice.

Columbus sends his sailors to find samples of new plants and animals while the leaders continue to barter for gold bracelets and ornaments. The surgeon is also the botanist for this trip and informs his leader that they have found Chinese rhubarb. Delighted with this discovery, Christopher continues to question the Indians about the ruler of China, Kublai Khan. The Arawaks nod agreement saying "Cuba-nacan" (meaning middle-Cuba), and they point inland.

After further consultations, Rodrigo de Jerez steps forward. "Who will join me to go to Cuba-nacan? We will

199

take food for five days and arms. It may be dangerous for another tribe of Indians has often attacked these people. But perhaps we will find the Khan and gold."

Several men volunteer.

Columbus selects ten, and orders, "Luis, you will go to translate and take my letter to the great Khan."

Martin Pinzón is becoming impatient. He has traded for a gold bracelet and a fine gold mask. Now he calls his small crew to return to the Pinta, but as he leaves, he grabs a zemis of gold from a noble's house. Once his skiff is secured on the Pinta, Martin Pinzón orders his crew on deck.

"Men, we are going to get more gold!"

"Sí, yes, yes," they respond.

"Then let's go! Half the gold we find will go to the crew. We will look for gold, not just ask for it. Pull up the anchor."

"Shall we tell Colón we are going?" Francisco Pinzón asks his brother.

"Leave him to his prayers. It is Sunday, so he will try to turn the Indians from their idols." Pinzón holds up the gold *zemis*, "See, I am helping him!"

The Pinta sails away.

Tuesday

The Treaty of Êtaples, signed by Henry, is presented to Charles. He adds his signature. When Henry's advisors collect the gold, they are also rewarded with generous gifts. Familiar with Henry's frugal ways, they are astonished by Charles' magnanimity. Charles feels victorious. The English have come to him, and they are taking their army home.

Jean Baptiste Poyet observes the signing and makes some sketches of Charles in his robes of state. Poyet is a favorite artist of the King and Queen in Tours, which is renowned for artists who illuminate manuscripts. Although they mainly produce prayer books, Poyet, Jean Bourdichon and others are not in monastic life.

Anne's prayer book shows her kneeling at confession, the scene bordered with gilded A's, N's, and E's. Anne was surprised to see her name used so decoratively; Poyet's flower borders are brilliant in pattern and fidelity to nature.

For Charles' prayer book, Poyet showed him kneeling between the Resurrected Christ and Mary Magdalene. They are in a lovely garden, enclosed by a fence which stretches toward the trees and mountains in the distance. Charles admires the sense of space and territory the artist conveys.

The young monarchs are almost old-fashioned, or very French, in preferring the exquisitely hand-lettered and illuminated books created by the artists of Tours. Let Henry's printers at Westminster produce hundreds of common printed books. Let him keep them across the channel. Charles and Anne can afford quality.

201

Anne of Brittany at Confession by Jean Baptiste Poyet, from her prayer book. Reproduced by courtesy of the Pierpont Morgan Library, New York. M. 250, f.14.

Wednesday

Returning to the coast from Cuba-nacan, Rodrigo and Luis report seeing shorter Indians who wore colorful leg bindings but soon began shooting arrows at them. A few blasts from the Spanish muskets and the Caribs had disappeared into the jungle. The inland party returns without meeting Khan and without gold, but they have some colorful parrots in cages and some large leaves from the tobacco plant.

After reporting to Columbus, Rodrigo challenges the other Spaniards, "Look at this big green leaf. What do you think the Indians use it for?"

The men are relaxed among the friendly Arawaks and guess:

"For a plate?"

"No," counters a sailor, "it is more the size of a platter."

"To cover their naked bodies?"

"As a hat, against the sun?"

Rodrigo enjoys their ignorance, as do the Arawaks. He teases, "After they use the leaf for a hat, it is dry and brown, like these we have brought. When it is set on fire, it burns very slowly."

The surgeon ventures, "Do they use it like a punk to start fires?" The most learned men of Europe have nothing to compare to tobacco.

The Arawaks are jubilant as they join Luis and Rodrigo to demonstrate. Rolling a large dry leaf tightly, a nobleman lights one end with a stick brought from a fire. He puts the other end to his nose. Blocking the other nostril

203

with a finger, he inhales deeply. The Indian expels the smoke through his nose and mouth. He offers his tobacco to Columbus, who defers to the surgeon. He puffs with his nostril, puffs again and coughs vigorously, much to the amusement of the Indians. With red eyes and a runny nose, he pronounces the tobacco safe to try.

Soon, the rolled leaves are circulating among the sailors. Some find their mouth is more effective than a nostril for keeping the ash burning. The Indians laugh as some of the white skins look a bit green. After months of bouncing around on the ocean, it's odd for sailors to get nauseous on land.

1st day of Ramadan, 897 A.H.

Rustam Shah, the Caliph of Persia has some cold partridge meat, bread, and several cups of goat milk in the pre-dawn darkness. Every day of the twenty-eight days of the month of Ramadan, Moslems everywhere abstain from all food and drink, and also from sexual relations, from sunrise to sundown. The purpose is to purify oneself physically by foregoing worldly comforts.

Rustam's third wife, KARAF, is pregnant, so she is excused from the fast, as are nursing mothers, children, and the elderly. Travelers are excused too, but all who are able are expected to make up the fast days at another time of the year or, if they cannot do that, feed a poor person a day for each fast day they have missed.

This first day of Ramadan is the hardest. Some Persians awake from sleep when the sun is up and find the thirst they feel more painful than the hunger. Still, they can thank God for many things. Persian Shiite Moslems are glad that Rustam Shah has gained control this year, ending two years of civil war since the death of Jaqub. The White Sheep party and the Black Sheep party have rivaled each other since the death of the great Timur[41] ninety years ago.

Timur left a fine observatory at Samarkand and a beautifully tiled mosque at Herat. The ancient Persian capital at Persepolis is still majestic in its ruins, but Ramadan reminds the rich and the poor, the powerful and the weak, that God controls the sunrise and the sunset. By observing the fast, the wealthy learn compassion for the poor and thankfulness for their blessings.

205

KARAF has been in labor all day. The women of the harem have been wiping her head with cool water and encouraging her. Now it is time to call a doctor. The al-Din family has provided physicians to the royal family and also medical books on circulation and illnesses. The best source on gynecology is still the 200 year old treatise by Sa'd al-Kalib or Cordoba.

Since this year Ramadan falls on the shorter, cooler days, the doctors don't find so many cases of heat prostration, but they too fast during the 10 1/2 hours of daylight and often cannot rest during the day.

After the sun sets, Rustam Shah is served a delicious meal with many bottles of water. He is also informed that his wife, KARAF, has delivered a healthy daughter.

Saturday and the 3rd day of Ramadan, 897 A.H.

Although Saxony has fine farm land, its wealth comes from mining silver, coal, lead, tin and copper. The Elbe River, starting from the forested mountains, links this industry to Hamburg and the Oceanvs Germanicvs (The Baltic and North Seas). The Luthers are not wealthy. Martin's father, a miner who has bought two copper smelting furnaces, has higher aspirations for his son. Duty and diligence are rewarded with further responsibilities.

Since it is Saturday, Martin is home from his school in Magdeburg. A book would make a fine birthday gift, pleasing the practical parents and the boy. Martin seems interested in law as a career, but he is also fond of music, singing in the church choir and caroling at the homes of the rich to earn money. The money is saved for his education.

His party will be a humble affair, some special apple kuchen and milk in a dark miner's house. Not like the elegant dinner last Spring for Michelangelo's seventeenth year at Lorenzo the Magnificent's villa in Florence.

Perhaps you would rather attend the party in Samarkand on the plains of central Asia. The tiled and marble tombs, mosques, and palaces still reflect the glory of Timur, the founder. In the sister city of Herat, science flourishes with a superior library and observatory. Baber, also nine, may receive a book from his father, the Sultan Husein ibn-Baigard, but he is hoping for a pony.

Baber will become the last of the Mongol Timured dynasty, losing political control, but in his flight, taking

207

the arts and education of his people to found the Mogul dynasty in India, building and ruling in Moslem Delhi.[42] At 39, he will be Babar, Zahir ud-Din Muhammad, and Martin Luther, released from prison at Wartburg, will be establishing the Reformed Christian church based on the

> *You're invited to a birthday party.*
> *Place: Eisleben, Saxony   Time:Saturday afternoon*
> *Martin Luther is nine years old.*

priesthood of all believers.

Sunday

Messengers arrive in Calais with 745,000 gold crowns and the Treaty of Étaples signed by Charles of France. Henry VII of England has been waiting on the continent; he is a practical man and satisfied with the terms. Even though he is supervising the withdrawal of his troops, he counts himself the victor. To rule England is his first priority; Charles' gold will help.

Henry hopes that Charles will kill Perkin Warbeck. It would save him the cost of an army to fight this pretender to his throne. This imposter is not, as he claims, Prince Richard of York. The spirit of that dead child has been troubling Henry's dreams. He felt powerless to protect his wife's younger brother at the time he was imprisoned in the Tower and killed. Perhaps the death of his mother-in-law has rekindled those sad memories. Henry resolves to use the gold to bolster England and his dynasty.

When the Great Harry sails up the Thames next week, Henry, like Charles in France, expects to be received as a victor. Of course, if King Richard hadn't killed his two nephews, Henry would not be king now. The old hunchback had some uses after all. Henry's claim to the throne was tenuous at best. Only the fact that the Yorks and Lancasters had slaughtered each other over a thirty year period put him anywhere near the top. And he married the last York to be on the safe side. Now that his mother-in-law is dead, that is one less expense. Henry brightens up considerably.

209

Friday

The Pinta continues its search for gold. Martin Pinzón, the captain, has named a river he discovered for himself. Now that the three ships have crossed the ocean sea, his resentments toward Colón have become outright rebellion. It is natural for the ships to be separated for a time at sea, but Martin is willfully disobeying in separating himself from the others. He goads his men to find gold at all costs.

Last night, Pinzón abruptly had decided to sail when the Caribs they had fired upon attempted to retaliate. These fierce Indians prey upon their Arawak neighbors. They kidnap their girls, rape them, and keep them captive to bear them children. The boy victims are castrated so they will grow fat. Then the Caribs kill them and eat them. Arawaks call them "Canibo", people eaters.

Now among the more peaceful Indians, the men of the Pinta are not much better than the Canibo. They rape and kill, loot and pillage, looking for gold and venting their anger. The stories Columbus told them of whole roofs of gold have not proven true. They are searching for gold and inspiring fear and hatred.

Christopher Columbus writes in his log, "As for monsters, I have found no trace of them except at one point on the second island on the way to the Indies. It is inhabited by a people considered throughout the islands to be most ferocious."[43] He has yet to reencounter Martin Pinzón.

Thanksgiving

The proud chief of the Susquehannas wears a bear-skin cloak that is much more than a cushion against the cold. A bear's head is positioned on each of his shoulders like giant epaulettes. The chief's arms extend through the mouth of each bear, but the sharp teeth are no longer any danger to the seven foot tall leader. The bears' claws hang at his back. The chief appears invincible. His people fish in the Chesapeake Bay and cultivate vast fields of corn, having brought this skill north from their ancestors the mound builders. On the west coast, Indians gather acorns for food and burn their brush shelters regularly when the fleas become too numerous. The Indians of North America live in varied surroundings, speak different languages and dialects, and have an unwritten history as complex as the recorded one of Europe.

The harvest has been gathered. The people are thankful that the Great Spirit has given them good crops of corn, squash, and peanuts. From the Delawares to the Natchez, a bountiful feast of Thanksgiving culminates the harvest season.

The Narragansetts, north of the Delawares, add a clam bake to their feast, but have to trade with the People called Seminole for pineapple and avocados. These are a rare delicacy in the north, often only sampled on trading trips. Large canoes travel the rivers, the main avenues through the dense forests. With a cold snap in the air, the Narragansetts retreat to their round wooden houses covered with elm bark. The shorter, colder days are a time for women to tan and fringe deerskin garments and decorate

211

them with porcupine quills. The men use snow shoes to pursue with bow and arrows the deer and turkey. The Narragansetts do not have tomatoes in such abundance as their Algonquin cousins to the south, but they have maple sugar and maple syrup stored in pots from last spring.

All along the Atlantic coast and west to the Mississippi River, more than 40 nations of people live in harmony with nature, if not always in harmony with each other. Although dialects differ, most people of the Eastern Forests share a common language, Algonquian. West of the great Mississippi River, the language of the Arapaho and the Cheyenne is also Algonquian. Sometimes they use sign language to communicate with neighboring tribes. They hunt the buffalo with spears, but their nomadic existence and trade is not far ranging, because the horse is unknown throughout the Americas.

Most tribes have an oral history, but few include their people coming from the east, over the land and islands in the north.[44] The different languages are evidence of many waves of migration. Most trace their beginnings to the Great Spirit making all plants and animals and men. Their chants and dances encourage them to live in harmony with nature, and to be thankful. The Delawares express their thanks with a harvest feast of corn, apples, peanuts, squash, and turkey.

Susquehannock, bronze sculpture, 1990, by Jud Hartmann, Blue Hill, Maine, based on the *Works of Capt. John Smith* published 1630.

213

December

Wednesday

After seven weeks on the island he has named
Fernando, Columbus sails south and in one day reaches a
verdant land he names Isabella. "I saw many trees very
different from ours and among them some that had
branches of many kinds and all on one trunk, thus on a
single tree there were five or six forms, all different." The
orchids are like nothing in Spain.

Juan de la Cosa, Columbus's second in command,
draws sketches of the plants that cannot be transported. He
has been an ideal assistant, carefully charting the land they
visit and always knowledgeable about the Santa Maria,
since it was originally his ship. He reports to Columbus,
"Martin Pinzón has already been here, and the men are
saying he and his men have been terrorizing the Indians
in their lust for gold."

"Mother of God!" Columbus shouts, "Pinzón has been
difficult from the start, but this has been real
insubordination. I should execute him!"

"Of course, you are right," Juan agrees, "As
commander, you have every right to kill him for disobeying
orders. I have known Martin all my life. He is an arrogant
and difficult man, but there is no one here who can better
sail the Pinta; we are three ships almost 3,000 miles from
Palos."

"Bring him to me, and we will see," Columbus
considers.

215

1st day of Shawwal, 897 A.H.

At the crossroads of central Africa, some people are celebrating Eid-al-Fitr, the feast following the last day of the fasting month of Ramadan. The followers of Islam are spending time with family, eating and celebrating. No intoxicating drinks are served, for this is always forbidden by the Koran. Enthusiasm leads some men to think of starting for Mecca for the Hajj.

"You had better start today," advises one Hajji, the title given to a man who has completed the once in a lifetime pilgrimage to Mecca. "It was a long trip last year, and very tiring. If some young Arab hadn't offered me a ride on his camel, I might never have arrived at the Kaaba. Of course, if I had died there, now I would be in paradise, at an even better party than this one."

This is the family of Askia Mohammed, ruler of the Songhoy Empire. These tall negroid peoples were converted to Islam more than 400 years ago, and Askia Mohammed is moving them to their greatest period of political power.

Another black culture, the Mandingo kingdom once flourished here, but now is reduced in size. The Mandingo king was also converted to Islam, but, like the Songhoy, not all his people were convinced. Everyone enjoys a feast, though, and as the celebration and eating in the sunlight extends to neighbors and acquaintances in the next few days, many who did not participate in the fast will enjoy the celebrating.

Some Mandingos have resisted Islam because of its strong aversion to idol worship. Beautiful bronze statues

216

of Mandingo Kings have been treasured for centuries as signs of culture and power. If the old ways were good and beautiful, why should one change?

Five years ago, the Portuguese came to Timbuktu, not coming up the Niger River, for it is not navigable this far north; the Portuguese came overland from the west. Their Christian ways are new in central Africa. They too fast and feast, but they also admire the bronze statues.

Everyone can enjoy the end of Ramadan, but the Songhoys enjoy it most.

Friday

Isabella and Fernando have held court in all parts of Spain. Their marriage joined the territories of Castile and Aragon. Their victory over the Moors added Granada, but their presence in all parts of their country has cemented their power. In Barcelona, Fernando is making a show of strength in the northeast for the benefit of his negotiations with Charles VIII of France. Charles seems most concerned that the Spanish heirs not be involved in marriage alliances with the children of Henry VII of England or with Maximillian, whose elderly father Frederick is King of Bohemia in name only. Fernando will make Charles pay with territory for such a concession.[46] Fernando believes such promises are made to be broken.

The royal children were all born in different parts of Spain. Isabel, the widow of the Prince of Portugal was born 22 years ago in Dueñas, a rather isolated city in Castile. After many miscarriages and still births, Juan was born in Sevilla, and a year later Juana, 13, was born in Toledo. The Queen sees that these older children study Latin with a scholarly woman, to prepare them for the very marriages that their father is denying. Isabella is reading Aesop's Fables to the younger girls. Maria, 10, was born in Cordoba with a twin who died in infancy. Seven-year-old Catalina was born when the court was at Alcala de Henares. The girls laugh at the story of the proud crow who opens his mouth when his singing is praised, and loses his meat. Aesop's stories have been printed in Castilian and illustrated with woodcut prints, thanks to the Queen's efforts in encouraging the printers in Zaragosa.

218

Juan and Juana come bursting in. "Mother, let me read to Maria and Catalina," Juana offers.

"Anything would be better than the lesson 'La Latina' has been forcing us to learn," Juan complains.

Before this interruption settles, a lady in waiting appears and asks the children to leave. Her look is so anguished that all are concerned.

"I am not a child," says the teen-aged Prince.

The lady-in-waiting is pale and flustered and stammers, "Hernand del Pulgar has an important message for you, my Queen."

"Send him in," Isabella replies. "Children, you may stay, but you must be quiet," the Queen instructs.

Hernand, the Queen's trusted secretary, kneels at her feet. "I bring sad news. As the King sat in court this morning to judge grievances, a crazed man sliced him with a sword. He lives, but he is seriously injured."

Maria starts to cry. Catalina remembers her mother's instructions and bites her lip.[47]

"Are the doctors with him? Where is he wounded?" Isabella asks.

"The doctors think they have stopped the bleeding," the secretary replies. "The sword grazed his head and ear and cut into his shoulder four fingers deep."

"Children, we must pray right now that God will spare your father, if it is His will." Isabella's mind races "Why did Fernando go to court," she thinks. "He enjoys riding and chess; he might have left this duty to others. All these years of fighting the Moslems, and he was never hurt. Now when he is 40..."

The Queen realizes she is arguing with God and turns to Him for peace and comfort.

Monday

The people of Haiti are handsome, peaceable, and eager to trade. Columbus notes in his log that they bring "parrots in cages, spun cotton in a skein, spears and many other things, and they exchanged them with us for other objects like little glass beads and bells."[48]

Columbus continues to collect for Isabella and Fernando: gold, pearls, spices, gum mastic, cotton, aloe wood. Also, he has promised to bring slaves.

These Indians resist coming aboard the Santa Maria, but Columbus locks twelve of them below deck, reasoning that when they reform from their idol worship, they will thank him for saving their souls. Their friends and families feel differently. They have carved mahogany boats which hold 150 people; they encircle the Santa Maria tied at anchor. These Indians who seemed so peaceful have bows and arrows and attempt a rescue. The sailors fire muskets and cannons. As the Indians tend to their wounded, the Santa Maria lifts anchor and sails away with twelve slaves.

Martin Pinzón has received a reprimand. Knowing he will not receive sterner punishment, he disappears again with the Pinta.

Today Pomo is a man. In two weeks of festivities, he has acquired a new name, a new loin cloth, and his first earrings.

The yearly celebration begins at the shrine of Huanacauri, where Pomo and the other boys each sacrifice a llama and pray, asking the god of the rock for permission to have the puberty rites. Once the gods agree, Pomo and the other boys are presented at the Temple of the Sun by their fathers. The ceremony takes place amid golden altars, fountains and finely wrought containers, some weighing 60 pounds, all of 18 carat gold. It is a privilege to be in the rooms of the temple and also the Garden of the Sun where all nature is reproduced in gold: corn, trees, birds, even butterflies of gold with emerald and turquoise accents.

Pomo's mother ignores the gold because she is so proud of her son and husband. She has worked many months spinning and weaving alpaca wool and sewing their special clothing. As she worked, she remembered her son as a baby, snugly tied in his cradle board. His arms were not freed for months, so they would be strong. She nursed him three times a day dangling her breast over the wooden cradle, but never holding him. When he was almost two, he was named and allowed to walk. Now at fourteen, he has had four years of schooling, one each in language, history, religion, and the quipu knot system of record keeping.

During the two week celebration, Pomo and the other boys are beaten to strengthen them, they dance, they drink *chicha* corn beer and sleep off its effects. They make

221

another pilgrimage to the sacred stone at Huanacauri for more beatings, dances and animal sacrifices. From there, they have a long downhill run, where several of the boys lose control and fall. Pomo reaches the end uninjured, and a noble girl presents him with yet another cup of *chicha*.

After some ritual bathing and more new clothes, Pomo has his ears pierced and the large ear plugs inserted which mark him a noble and a warrior. His uncle gives him a sling, mace and shield. Other relatives also give him gifts and lots of advice. In this structured society, he will not go through such an elaborate ceremony for another ten or eleven years, when he marries.

Monday, Christmas Eve

Yesterday at sea, Christopher started reading his old Latin manuscript of the Gospel of Luke. It begins before Jesus was born; first God sent the infant John the Baptist to Elizabeth and Zachariah so he could prepare the way for the Saviour. Columbus planned to give his men two days of rest to celebrate the Nativity, and he hoped to inspire them with this story. Perhaps they could identify with John the Baptist, the one who goes first to prepare the way.

But last evening, everything changed when they went ashore. The Indian Chief Guacanagari was quite emphatic that gold was to be found at Cibao. Cibao must be the Indian pronunciation for Cipangu, Japan, and it is near.

So this has been a day at sea. Before first light, the sails are set and the Niña and the Santa Maria pull up anchor. Now Columbus dreams of celebrating Christmas dinner with the Emperor of Japan, eating food from thick plates of gold under a golden roof. But the winds have not cooperated. The smaller Niña has made slow progress and the Santa Maria even less.

After the sun sets, the men sing songs of Christmas and enjoy an extra ration of wine. The air is calm and the sea is like glass. No need to set the anchor. A weary Columbus leaves a boy at the tiller and goes to his cabin for some sleep.

Tuesday, Christmas

Christmas begins with morning Mass, made more joyful as the choir boys vigorously shake and beat tambourines to accompany their soprano voices. Some look sleepy because late last night they were parading around town with a couple dressed like Mary and Joseph. Mary rode a donkey and Joseph knocked on doors and asked for a room; they were turned away. The singing that accompanied them floated up to the balconies and windows.

In church, the Baby Jesus doll carved of wood is wearing a silk dress, little gold shoes, and a golden crown. As mass ends, the Bishop brings the Christ Child to Isabella, and she kisses it tenderly. Then all are invited to come forward and kneel and kiss the charming statue. No one is in a hurry to leave. Christmas gifts will be exchanged in two weeks when the church celebrates the three kings bringing gifts to Jesus. Isabella hopes her new court painter, Miguel Sithium, will complete a Madonna and child as lovely as those of his teacher, Memling of Bruges, for her gift to Fernando.

The Bishop adds a closing prayer, "Thank you God that our King Fernando is healing well. Thank you that the Moslems have been defeated. Thank you God for the Jews who have been converted. And thank you for the birth of our Savior, Jesus Christ."

Isabella adds a petition in her heart, "Dear God, be with Cristóbal Colón and his men and bring them safely home from China."

The Queen has appointed all the bishops of Spain for the last ten years. This one should have remembered the Enterprise of the Indies in his prayers. She will remind him. The Catholic Church in Spain is a reflection of Isabella's piety and strength; she has prevailed against the Pope on the issue of appointing bishops. She is thankful that God has spared Fernando. But if God had willed her husband should die, He would also give her the strength to rule.

Tuesday, Christmas

Sunrise in Barcelona is midnight in the Caribbean. Isabella's prayers are timely. At just that hour, the Santa Maria, with a boy at the tiller, runs into a coral reef. The initial crunch wakes Columbus, but not everyone. He orders some men to take the skiff to assess the damage and attempt to free his ship. The wind has finally come up, an offshore flow which pushes the Santa Maria more and more onto the coral.

"Lower the sails," he orders. The wind no longer buffets the ship, but the tide is going out, and she sinks further and further into her coral trap. All of the crew of forty are awake now and begin to bring everything above deck and load the skiff for trips to shore. The cannon-shot ballast is thrown overboard. If they lighten the load, they may yet get their ship to float free. Next the barrels of wine are tossed; they will float.

At the first light of dawn, the Santa Maria is taking on water and the tide is beginning to rise. The only encouraging sight is a group of rescue boats. In eighteen hours at sea, the flagship has only traveled two miles. Guacanagari has seen the problem and sends help. The Indian boats make many round trips from the crippled ship to shore. All the men are saved and most of the cargo. Soon, the rising tide floods the hold and washes some of the barrels towards shore.

Juan de la Cosa sees the ship that was like a son to him break apart on the reef. The main mast still stands tall, but the bow and mizzen masts are angling towards the beautiful blue water. Each surge of the tide wrenches the Santa Maria until more planks are floating, and just a skeleton of the flagship creaks and moans on the reef in the noonday sun.

Friday

Anne of Brittany prays for her husband's health. The Chapel at Amboise is cold, but she is wearing a wool shawl over her fine wool dress, and the candles give a warm glow. Across the courtyard, Charles is by a fireplace; the chill he received hunting has turned into an alarming congestion in his chest. She opens her prayer book to the section on saints. "Saint Comé and Saint Damien, come and purge Charles of all illness and restore him to full strength and vigor," she prays. Pictured is Comé holding a urinal and Damien with a faience jar with medicines. Yes, one must pray, and one must also act. She will prepare a poultice of mustard on parchment for Charles' chest. And yes, Charles must drink some herbal waters; the sight of the urinal reminds her that he need lots of liquids, but also that she misses their wedding bed. Blushing that her thoughts could be so erotic in a chapel, she turns the parchment pages of her Book of the Hours and stops at St. Hubert, the hunter who saw a vision of the crucifix in a stag's horns. If one's thoughts must wander, best let them go to holy thoughts. "Mea culpa," she whispers.

Anne decides to gather the mustard blossoms herself. Emerging from the chapel, she can see their yellow carpeting the ground among the dormant grape vines. Wrapping her shawl around her bosom, she found Lady JANINE at her side. A bracing walk among the mustard is just what Anne needs to clear her head.

Charles' determination to be drawn into a conflict with Naples puzzles her. It seems the Duke of Milan is just flattering him, encouraging him to fight their mutual enemy. Charles would risk much more than the Sforza family. Yet, when his health returns, he will probably march to the south and exert his claim over Naples. If God would send them a healthy child, perhaps Charles would be more content at home.

Returning with the mustard blossoms, JANINE suggests that the cook prepare a poultice, while they enjoy a game of cards; Anne agrees. Charles will get expert care, and the 52 cards hold a fascination for her; all the Kings, Ladies and Knaves battling for their suit. It is just a game, but isn't this life also like a game, preparing one for eternal life.

Sunday

Savonarola continues to preach against worldliness and immorality, and the people of Florence crowd into San Marco to hear him. So uncompromising is his view of the gospel, that Pope Alexander VI has reluctantly permitted him to remove his monastery from the jurisdiction of the Dominican hierarchy in Lombardy.[50] Savonarola had predicted that Lorenzo de Medici and the Pope would die this year, and his prophecy proved true. His congregation wonders what he will predict for 1493. The reformer answers only to God, but dictates fearlessly to Rome and to the weak Piero de Medici, who tries to rule Florence.

Zealous young reformers are joining his independent monastic order. They wear the Dominican robes, but their devotion is to the God that Savonarola knows so intimately. They obey their vows of celibacy and poverty. Savonarola sells gold chalices and patens to buy food for the poor. Many wealthy people respond to his example, donating their pagan jewels to his charities and burning their immoral art and books to purify themselves.

The beautiful Virgin Mary and child that Sandro Botticelli painted behind the altar looks down on the artist and the throngs of people who listen in stunned silence as Savonarola continues to predict more disasters.

"God will not tolerate the Pope's whore in Rome. He will not overlook the sinful life that Piero de Medici lives." Savonarola casts his eyes to heaven and sighs, "God will bring destruction on them, and on all sinners."

Botticelli longs for the beauty of heaven. The monk's words are frightening and especially alarming because his past predictions have proven true.

"When God sends the Christian leader of His choosing to Florence, there will be destruction. Many will die. Are you ready to die?" Savonarola sees fear in some eyes and tears in others. He continues in a low voice, "I am ready to die. And, I am ready to stand along side Christ as he rules Florence.[51] God has shown me that I must die a violent death for His sake. I willingly die to purify his church."

No one speaks, but their hearts are saying, "No, no!" How can they forestall this terror?

"Do not go to brothels and gambling halls; pray to God and help the poor and weak," the sermon continues. "Don't buy indulgences from Rome and then continue to sin. Resolve in this new year to live to the honor and glory of Jesus Christ."

Monday

Columbus had planned to continue exploring for another two or three months; he is sure these islands are just off the coast of China. The loss of the Santa Maria has changed everything. The Niña had returned as soon as Vincente Pinzón realized he was alone, but his independent brother, Martin, and the Pinta may be anywhere, even breaking up on a coral reef.

Christopher's dismay at losing his ship has changed to acceptance and even joy.

"God meant for us to leave men here to teach the Indians about Him," he tells everyone who will listen.

This week has been a busy one. Guacanagari and his people have continued to help salvage boards and cannons from the coral reef. From the sea, they gathered kegs of wine, many planks, and even the masts after the ship broke apart. A sturdy fort is almost completed. Diego de Arana will be the leader for the thirty-eight men that must be left behind. Diego is the cousin of Beatriz, Christopher's mistress, who is caring for both of his sons. The sailors have been stocking the fort with salvaged food, arms and ammunition. Columbus has ordered the surgeon, tailor, and artillery specialist to stay at this first European colony in the New World.

Columbus and Juan de la Cosa have moved on to the Niña, and are preparing her to sail. Some ballast has been taken to the fort for ammunition, leaving more space for cargo. Gold, pearls, tobacco, corn and other plants are easily stowed. The living cargo is more complex. Several captured Indians have sickened and died in just a few months, and so have some of the beautiful Amazon parrots, especially those isolated in cages. Once their flying feathers were cut and these exotic birds were released from their cages, the naturally noisy parrots revived with companionship.

The hold of the tiny Niña is a microcosm of the New World occupied by forty parrots of great variety in size and color, and the Indians who value them as pets and as food. Luis de la Torre has begun teaching Spanish to six Indians, four men and two women.

"Repeat, please," Luis instructs. "I call myself Luis."

The Indians repeat, "I call myself..." adding their names.

"I am at your service," Luis directs.

The parrots screech, and a few imitate Luis.

"These birds learn quickly," he chides. "When we introduce you to the King and Queen, perhaps the parrot on your shoulder will be the first to say, 'Buenos días'."

Columbus is on deck. From the crow's nest comes news, the Pinta has been sighted on the horizon. Columbus wonders what treasures Martin Pinzón has in the hold of the Pinta; none realize that a fever some of the sailors have experienced is syphilis, which they are carrying back to an unsuspecting Europe. The two remaining caravels should meet in a few days to cross the ocean together. Columbus hopes that the riches he brings and those he dreams of bringing in the future will help Isabella and Fernando to send armies to Jerusalem and free it from the infidel. He must return here, not just for riches, but for his thirty-nine men.

Columbus lands once more at La Navidad to report to his men at the fort. He tells them, "We have sighted the Pinta. In a few days, we will both be sailing east. Your fort is strong; you have provisions for a year. Guacanagari

233

has promised he will live at peace with you. I thank God for every one of you, and assure you that I will return for you next year."

THE END

If, like Erasmus, we reckon that 1493 did not begin until March 25, then Columbus completed his first voyage in 1492. In a fierce storm on the night of February 13th, the Niña, with insufficient ballast, suffered extensive damage but miraculously survived to limp to shore at the Azores on February 15. Repairs there and at Lisbon took 20 days. The Pinta under Martin Pinzón was blown off course to the south, but both caravels arrived home at Palos on March 15.

Later Columbus traveled to Barcelona for a triumphal parade before Fernando and Isabella, who agreed to finance a second voyage of seventeen ships. True to his promise, Christopher Columbus returned to La Navidad in 1493; he found the fort in ruins, all the Spaniards dead and Guacanagari wounded, claiming he had tried to defend the Spanish against a hostile tribe.

Albrecht Dürer was asked to critique gold ornaments from the New World, and this great artist and son of a goldsmith pronounced the design and craftsmanship excellent, comparable to European work. Dürer also admired feather capes brought from the Americas, two of which remain in European museums; the early gold pieces are known only from descriptions, as the gold was recycled.

Charles VIII, encouraged by Ludovico Sforza, successfully invaded Naples in 1495-6, capturing Florence along the way. Savonarola welcomed him as God's judgement upon the city. For a short time the monk served on a Council of Rulers under Charles. He continued to defy Pope Alexander, refusing to cease preaching or to come to Rome. Savonarola was tried and convicted by a church court and hanged by civil authorities on May 24, 1498. Then his body was burned. Charles also died that year of fever, but Anne of Brittany continued to be the Queen of France. She married the new king, Louis XII, who obtained a quick divorce from his first wife. Columbus sailed on his third voyage just six days after Savonarola was executed, and, going south from the Caribbean islands, was the first European to set foot on an American continent.

Catalina of Aragon was betrothed to Prince Arthur of England. As she traveled there in 1499, she visited the pilgrimage church of Santiago de Compostella where the giant censer fell into the crowd injuring several, but not the princess. After the death of Arthur and his father Henry VII, Catalina became the first wife of Henry VIII, Queen Catherine.

In 1502, Pope Alexander borrowed an Army from the Duke of Urbino and then had his son Cesare attack the now defenseless Duchy. The Pope sold most of the Duke's art collection to finance further wars.

The Inca was succeeded by his son, Atahualpa, who eventually succumbed to Pizarro.

The Algonquins and their neighbors remained relatively undisturbed by the peripatetic Europeans for a century more.

Portuguese sailors were the first Europeans to reach Japan in 1543, followed by St. Francis Xavier in 1549. Shoguns continued to rule in the name of the Emperor. China remained secure in its vision of itself as the center of the universe for 151 more years of Ming emperors.

Hawaii and Australia had a few more centuries to themselves before Captain Cook "discovered" them.

Sub-Saharan Africa, the nearest uncharted land to the explorers of Europe was left until last. It was not untouched; many of its people were enslaved and taken west to tame the new lands. The civilizations of central Africa were in a period of decline by the time a new generation of the explorers reached the interior of the "Dark Continent".

Islam continued to advance in southern Asia reaching as far as the Philippines. The Moguls quickly become rulers of India, building palaces and forts and adding a rich new layer to Buddhist and Hindu traditions.

Europe was the most materially successful of continents, and also the most divided.

As the 1490s drew to a close, Spain was becoming the most powerful nation in Europe and was transplanting her culture and language across the Atlantic. But, addicted to American gold, she faltered, becoming a site for dynastic struggles and other people's wars.

In 1502, Columbus made his fourth and final voyage west, still insisting that he was at the doorstep of Japan and China. Nevertheless, his explorations were a seminal contribution which led the way for searches in all areas of human knowledge, and sparked an interchange of art and culture as great as any in our history.

[1] Calendars and dates varied greatly in 1492. The Mayans had the most accurate calendar. The Kingdom of the Kongo had a flourishing civilization but no calendar. Dates in Florence differed from those in Milan. The Julian calendar was used in Europe, and would be, in some places, for another 210 years. But just 90 years later, Pope Gregory dropped the ten days the calendar had acquired since the time of Julius Caesar. People went to bed on October 4, 1582, and awoke to October 15, 1582, bringing the dates back into harmony with the solar seasons. While Roman Catholic Europe made these changes, Protestant parts of Germany delayed until 1700 and Great Britain till 1752. Imperial Russia never did change; the USSR did in 1918. Turkey adopted the Gregorian calendar in 1928.

When we begin in January of 1492, in China, it is the year of the pig, with the lunar new year of the rat weeks in the future. The Mayans are in mid-year. The Hebrew year is 4252, an important and terrifying time for the Jewish communities that flourished in Spain. The Moslems are in the tenth month of 896. Their lunar calendar has 354 or 355 days to the year and makes no attempt to reconcile itself with the solar seasons.

[2] The Catholic Monarchs, a title granted by Pope Alexander in 1493.

[3] Calendar of Patent Rolls, February 1, 1492.

[4] AWATA is a fictional character. The names of fictional characters will appear in the small capital letters.

[5] Barbara Dürer's eighteenth child was born in 1494.

6 1. Rat; 2. Ox; 3. Tiger; 4. Hare; 5. Dragon; 6. Snake; 7. Horse; 8. Sheep; 9. Ape; 10. Cock; 11. Dog; 12. Pig

7 A.H. – Anno Hegirae, the western designation for Islamic years.

8 A picul is approximately 140 pounds.

9 The Angelus was rung at morning, noon and evening to celebrate the incarnation of Christ.

10 The 2½% donation to charity has replaced the duty of Holy War for some Moslems.

11 Over 2000 years before 1492, people lived at Sarum.

12 The stained glass windows have survived to 1990, the tomb was destroyed by Henry VIII, and Thomas removed from the list of Saints of the Church of England.

13 Some sources say 500,000 per year, which seems high given the population.

14 In gratitude to San Diego, Isabella and Ferdinand built a Pilgrim's Inn at Compostella in 1497. In 1499, Catalina visited on her way to England to marry the Prince, and the giant censer fell.

15 Mila, the Cotton Clad, is also referred to as Milarepa or Mi-la-ras-pa.

16 Slavery has been a part of human interaction for millennia and existed world-wide. Parents sell children; the vanquished in battle become slaves. Swedes captured Russians and sold them to Moslems. African tribes enslaved their neighbors. Portuguese brought the first cargo of 200 black African slaves to Lisbon in 1444. Later, Christopher and Bartolome Columbus made and sold charts to those who continued the slave trade. The caste system of India kept people in privilege or servitude. At the same time, provision for freedom and

239

full citizenship was also a part of many cultures. The Moslems practiced equality among believers, regardless of race or ethnic background.

Some Europeans used Aristotle's argument that nature intends for some men to be slaves; others disagreed. In the decades following Columbus's voyage, the American Indians were the focus of this debate.

[17] Qaitbay died July, 1494; Muhammed ruled to 1498.

[18] Twenty years later they deposed their father and fought each other. Selim had Ahmed executed after he was defeated.

[19] Sichel, *Women and Men of the French Renaissance*, p. 87.

[20] Better known as Titian outside of Italy. Titian claimed to be born in 1477, but recent scholarship now places his birth at 1487 or 1488. He died in 1576.

[21] Columbus first encountered the Mayans in 1502. Responding to questions about their buildings, the Mayans answered, "Ci-u-than", meaning "we don't understand you." This became Yucatan.

[22] The Mayans numbered their days starting with zero.

[23] In 1465.

[24] Mayans were the only New World people with a written language. Three pre-Columbian books survive in museums in Paris, Madrid and Dresden.

[25] Aborgine word translated "ourselves".

[26] The ducat is a gold coin of Venice, 24 carat gold, 3.559 grams. Obverse shows Doge kneeling, receiving a banner from St. Mark. Reverse shows Christ standing in an oval of stars, inscribed "sit tibi, Christe, dattus quem tu reges iste ducatas," hence ducat. The Latin

translates, "Let this duchy which thou rulest be dedicated to thee, O Christ." In 1990, the gold in 45,000 ducats would be worth $225,000.

[27] Erasmus, *Epistles* Vol II, p. 171.

[28] The 49 year old cardinal became Pope Julius II in 1503 and hired Michelangelo and Raphael to add frescoes to the Sistine Chapel and also began construction of St. Peter's.

[29] Earliest signed portrait by Giovanni Bellini, in Norton Simon collection.

[30] Jacob Fugger died childless in 1525.

[31] Chant recorded by Abraham Fornander (1812–1887).

[32] 16 gills equal 2 quarts. The wine was mixed with water to keep the water potable during the long voyage, so it was diluted by modern standards.

[33] 150–170 nautical miles

[34] 1200 feet

[35] Watling Island, The Bahama Islands

[36] The journal of Columbus was given to Isabella and Ferdinand, who presented him with a copy. Both of those books have been lost, but Las Casas' versions make fascinating, if not entirely accurate, reading. This quotation is rendered from the Columbus letter, probably written on his return voyage and sent to Barcelona when he arrived in Lisbon. It was translated into German in 1497. Cecil Janes' scholarly translation for the Hakluyt Society in 1929 is a definitive source.

[37] Pope Paul III (1534–1549)

[38] Margaret and Anton had 17 children.

[39] Gold coins marked with the crown of the monarch, of considerable buying power, prior to the influx of gold from the New World.

[40] On the death of Edward IV, 1483, his 12 year old son, Edward, became king, but a power struggle between regents resulted in Edward and his youger brother, Richard, being imprisoned in the Tower of London by their uncle Richard III. There was some mystery about the boys' deaths, and Perkin Warbeck, a commoner from Flanders, claims to be the young Richard.

[41] Timur (1336–1405), also known as Tamerlane, conquered and ruled much of Asia.

[42] When a Mongol goes to India he becomes a Mogul.

[43] See endnote 36.

[44] During the last ice age, 20,000 B.C., the Aleutian Islands provided that land bridge.

[45] Today, Haiti, Hispaniola

[46] The Treaty of Narbonne, January 19, 1493, Charles ceded Roussillon and Cerdagne to Fernando, hoping for his support in his war on Naples.

[47] Catherine of Aragon, pledged and married to Prince Arthur of England and after his death to Henry VIII, was stoic.

[48] See endnote 36.

[49] The Island of Hispaniola, Dominican Republic half.

[50] Actually happened in 1493.

[51] Savonarola was named to a new Signory which framed a constitution for Florence.